Praise for *Frances Finkel and the Passenger Pigeon*

"Mahoney throws light on the neglected contributions of female pilots in World War II. She conveys not just the importance of the work, but also its dangers and, often, its tremendous fun..."   —*Kirkus Reviews*

"It's brilliant to have books that shine a light on strong female lead characters and even better when these books are based in part on the female history and participation in the war, something not always taught in schools."

—*LoveReading (UK)*

"...A fabulous combination of an aviation professional using her aviation knowledge to create a unique work of fiction that showcases her writing skills and imagination. [Mahoney] has managed to use layman's terms such that no reader will feel lost in the narrative which is deftly executed."

—*Hollywood Book Review*

FRANCES FINKEL

AND THE

PASSENGER PIGEON

D.M. MAHONEY

Red Cardinal Writing (USA) LLC

Frances Finkel and the Passenger Pigeon is a work of historical fiction. The dialogue of any characters, real or otherwise, is entirely made up and does not necessarily reflect or represent the views or opinions held by individuals on which characters are based. A sincere effort was made to be consistent with the nature of any real person speaking, based on generally known facts of their lives and events that occurred while the story takes place.

Trade Paperback First Edition 2021

Published by Red Cardinal Writing

Copyright @ 2021 by D. M. Mahoney

Library of Congress Control Number: 2021919445

ISBN: 978-1-66781-458-2
ISBN: 978-1-66781-459-9 (eBook)

Printed in the United States of America

www.redcardinalwriting.com

I believe there is a common life force that desires
to help another, whatever the cost.

— D. M. Mahoney

FRANCES FINKEL

FINKEL

AND THE

PASSENGER

PIGEON

PART I

"Our destiny is not mapped out for us by some exterior power;
we map it out for ourselves. What we think and do in the
present determines what shall happen to us in the future."

— Christian D. Larson

CHAPTER 1

He's late again.

Fran stood up from the kitchen table to look out the window for her younger brother, who was due back from his paper route.

She opened the refrigerator and removed four raisin cookies, two apples and a sandwich. She placed the items into a small sack, grabbed her flight jacket from its hook by the front door and headed out to the hangar with the food.

The sun had burned off the fog from earlier that morning, and the sky was clear of clouds.

Perfect flying weather could be his saving grace.

Fran went into the hangar and headed over to her airplane. She did most of her flying in the trainer plane, and when she sat in the pilot's seat, she often wondered what had happened to its original owner.

Last summer, a young man landed at Seal Rock Airport in a new, yellow Piper J-3 Cub. He asked the Finkels to make him a fair offer for the plane as he was about to enlist in the army. They paid five hundred dollars to take the aircraft off the lad's hands. Their father chipped in one hundred to the four hundred Fran and her twin brother, Danny, had earned from cutting hay in the field next to the hangar. Their arms grew strong from shifting through the H-shaped gear shaft of the tractor, and that extra strength came in handy when they were flying.

Fran did a quick flight check of the aircraft before climbing into the cockpit. As she taxied along the dirt road that led to their house, she caught a glimpse of Seamus frantically pedaling his bike.

When she stopped the plane in front of their home, her brother and father were both in the doorway. Seamus grinned at her. Fran pressed down on the brakes and left the engine running as she waved him over. Seamus looked at his father for approval, who looked down at him over his glasses before nodding. Seamus gave him a quick hug before running towards the plane.

"But be careful!" their father shouted over the noise of the engine. "You stay clear of the propeller — and take that hat off!"

Seamus took off his newsboy cap and stuffed it into his pocket. "Thanks, Papa!" he shouted back.

Seamus waved to his sister, looking at her eyes to make sure she saw him. She had taught him to do so when approaching any idling aircraft. Fran nodded and gave him a thumbs-up. He came closer and noticed the sack of lunch on the passenger seat.

"Well, get in already!" she yelled over the sound of the engine.

Fran worried if Seamus were late one more time, they would hold him back a year, delaying his graduating high school. And that would mean he couldn't take over to help their father after she left.

Seamus grabbed his lunch and hopped in. After strapping on his seat belt, he opened the sack and peeked inside. He looked at his older sister and blew her a kiss.

Fran pressed down on the right rudder pedal and spun the plane around for a 180-degree sweep. She looked over the surrounding area — left, right, above and behind, then pushed the throttle forward as far as it would go. They were airborne in seconds as she deftly cleared the tall pines surrounding their home.

As soon as the plane lifted off the ground, Fran felt right at home. The first time she flew, and every time after that, she knew it was where she belonged.

Seamus was singing a medley to amuse her. It reminded her of how their mother would sing as she puttered around the house or cooked. Sometimes she simply hummed or whistled. Until Danny was gone. There wasn't any more humming or singing after that.

Their father changed as well. He used to be loud and opinionated, so intense — either ecstatic or infuriated. He became sullen. It was as if someone had snuffed the light out of him. Fran would listen to her parents murmuring behind closed doors late into the night. She couldn't make out the words of their hushed, irate whispering. Fran would have preferred loud, angry conversation or screaming, the throwing of things she could hear crash and break apart. Both parents were not the same. Neither was Fran. One change in her was even visible: after witnessing her brother's accident, she woke up the next day with an inch-wide streak of white in her long, dark hair.

Scarcely ten minutes had passed when they saw her brother's school below. She had a particular area that served well as a landing strip. Fran flew there and rolled to a stop so Seamus would make it to school on time.

He hopped out of the plane, and Fran watched him run towards the campus. She did not find the ornate and insular institution as impressive as her mother had.

Margaret Finkel enrolled Fran's brothers in the private school with the hope it would teach them how to behave fittingly in society. It was in their grandfather's will that a trust fund provided for the boys' education. Few colleges were accepting Jewish students. This would give them a foot in the door of those that did.

Since Fran was a girl, they assumed her future husband would take care of her financially.

As she began taxiing the plane for takeoff, she remembered when Danny had ridden his motorcycle to school.

"Master Finkel, we do not allow motorbikes here!" the headmaster had said after marching over to him, red-faced and furious.

The headmaster wasn't keen on having Danny enrolled in his school and would have happily expelled him. After being ordered off the school's premises, her brother kicked down hard to start the bike.

"No!" the headmaster roared. "No motor. You push that contraption out of here until you are off of school property."

Students had gathered around, and a crowd had formed. Humiliated, Danny hopped off the bike and pushed it down the road. A few boys snickered.

Fran pushed the throttle forward. The plane was much lighter without Seamus; it lifted quickly off the ground and into the air. However, instead of pulling back to gain altitude, she kept the plane level and headed straight for the school building. She only pulled back at the last second as the plane's wheels came within inches of the roof. The aircraft's vibration rattled the building, and a few shingles shook off from the plane's force.

Fran chuckled to herself. *I hope there aren't any rules about having airplanes buzz the school.*

When she returned home, she knew her father would be anxious. He didn't like both of his children out flying at the same time. Too much at stake if anything happened, Fran figured.

A mechanic nodded to her as he was opening the hangar doors. Her father was working on a bright blue Interstate Cadet, one of the trainer planes used for flight lessons. He smiled a strained smile when she taxied the Cub around him and stopped by the Stearman, another airplane waiting for Fran to take out for its test flight.

Fran always came straight home, so the wait wouldn't be too long for him. She wanted to ease her father's worry and let him know when she landed safely. She added that to her list of intentions to think about right before drifting off to sleep, when her waking thoughts moved into her subconscious. Fran wasn't sure how or why it worked, but she noticed when she wanted something in particular to happen, it did.

Somehow, unbeknownst to her, her thoughts were making their way out into the Universe.

CHAPTER 2

After a routine glance across the cockpit, Fran lifted her flight goggles and scowled at the oil gauge needle, waving erratically.

A row of pelicans darted over a cresting sea wave as she flew above them, the Stearman's yellow wings glaring in defiance against the blue sky.

It was warm for the first day of November 1941. Fran wiped the sweat from her forehead as she strained to listen to the whine of the engine. She banked the plane to the left and pushed the throttle forward to full power as she sped back to the airport. Ten long minutes crept by before she could see Seal Rock Airport on the horizon.

Fran heard the engine sputter, then stop. The silence startled her.

Perfect timing, she thought as she shook her head. Fran held the plane's nose level, looked left and right for any nearby aircraft, flipped the ignition switch to the off position, then headed straight towards the runway.

The windshield was covered with oil, forcing Fran to lean out of the plane so she could see. Black smoke billowed out from the engine as she slipped the plane down onto the airstrip. She pressed her feet on the brakes, bringing the smoking plane to a stop.

One of the mechanics ran over with a fire extinguisher and began to spray the plane's engine. Fran pulled herself up and out of the cockpit, then stepped onto the wing before jumping down, her boots hitting hard on the paved runway.

"Say, you all right, Fran?" the gangly mechanic asked.

"Yes, I'm fine, Skeeter," she said, coughing.

When she lifted up her goggles, there were light rings around her eyes. The rest of her face was smudged black from smoke. Fran swept back her hair and saw her father waving his arms as he sprinted across the runway towards her.

"Engine quit?" he asked, trying to catch his breath.

She nodded.

Fran was one of the mechanics at her father's shop. She was also his only flight test pilot.

"Probably shot," she said as they watched Skeeter spray the front of the plane. "It's a shame. That Stearman is a good trainer plane. The student pilots just beat on it too much."

"I was afraid of that. I knew you shouldn't have taken it out. What if — "

"Papa," Fran said, cutting him off. "I'm glad it happened to me and not a student or a customer. I know what to do when there's a problem. I'm going to clean up and start dinner. We can work on the engine tomorrow."

She began the mile-long walk towards their house, then stopped.

"Thank you, Skeeter!" she yelled over her shoulder.

He stopped spraying the extinguisher and waved.

"Oh sure, Fran!" he said, blushing. "Anything for you!"

Skeeter was sweet and a hard worker, but he was also painfully shy. He hadn't spoken over two sentences to Fran in the five years she had known him.

She stopped at the end of their driveway to check the mailbox. Fran was waiting for her *Popular Aviation* magazine to arrive. She also enjoyed her mother's *Ladies Home Journal* and *Women's Home Companion*. The post office still delivered both magazines to the house, even though Mrs. Finkel no longer lived there.

Fran scoured each publication, searching for any mention of a female pilot. She knew there must be other women pilots out there in the world. Only she hadn't heard of any besides Amelia Earhart, who was now missing.

However, last month Fran stumbled across a tribute to Harriet Quimby. She was the first female to earn a pilot's license and the first woman in the United States to have her driver's license and own a car.

Fran yearned to be the first to do something. To feel significant.

She hadn't mentioned the article to anyone. Her brothers would tell her there weren't any other women pilots and tease her about it. Their father would roll his eyes at the notion of a professional female pilot.

Her mother also thought it was ridiculous. But Fran thought if she was a famous female pilot, perhaps her mother would change her mind and even brag about her to her friends. She'd be proud of her daughter then, or at least be able to look at her again since Danny's accident.

There was no mail that day.

Fran sighed and went into the house. She washed her face and combed her hair before heading to the kitchen and putting on an apron. She planned to make a fish chowder and was peeling potatoes when her younger brother came into the kitchen. He crept over to the jar of cookies behind her and took one out, then stuffed it into his mouth.

"Seamus, you're going to ruin your appetite," Fran said with her back to him.

"So?" he said with his mouth full. "You're not my mother. You can't tell me what to do."

He took out another cookie, then grudgingly placed it back in with the others.

"Fran, I swear you have eyes in the back of your head."

Seamus leaned against the kitchen counter. He was almost 15 but short for his age, which made him appear much younger. At five feet, eight inches, Fran towered over him. She was tall, like their mother — a striking woman with auburn hair and hazel eyes.

She'd disappeared a few months ago, up and left the day after Fran graduated from high school. Mrs. Finkel was an excellent cook, and she taught Fran everything about running the household. As if she knew she was going to leave. As if she planned it all along.

"Here, cut these for me, please," Fran said, placing the peeled potatoes in front of Seamus. "Make yourself useful."

She pushed his hair back from his forehead and looked into his eyes.

"You need a haircut."

"How did the Stearman flight test go?"

"Don't ask," she said while reaching under the counter to take out a large pot for the chowder. She took out two more, along with a pan. She filled one with water and lit all four burners on the old O'Keefe stove. Soon she would have something cooking on each of them. Fran moved swiftly and meticulously in the kitchen, as she did when working in her father's shop.

"Was that what the smoke was from?" Seamus said as he delicately chopped potato into small squares. "I could see it out my bedroom window."

"Most likely. The engine failed."

"Were you flying?"

"Yes, I was."

"Weren't you afraid?" he asked.

"Nah, if you know what to do, you can land safe and sound, even without an engine. That's as long as you don't have a fire in the cockpit. Then you're in trouble."

"Fran, what if there was a fire?" he asked. "What if something happened to you?"

"If there were a fire, I would jump out of the plane," she said. She placed the fish into the pan. "That's why I wear a parachute, silly goose."

She squeezed his neck. "Don't you worry about me. Nothing is going to happen to me, okay?"

"Say...you know...it's almost here."

"What's that?"

"Ah, quit teasing me. You know darn well in two more days I'll be fifteen."

She did. She also knew Seamus wanted a kitten for his birthday, and she planned to surprise her younger brother with one.

Every day over the last several weeks, Seamus read Fran all the newspaper ads for free kittens. There seemed to be a proliferation of litters in nearby towns along the Oregon Coast. And this only fueled his kitten fever.

"I asked the folks on my route if they knew anybody who had kittens," he had told her. "Lots of people said they did."

Fran didn't respond. They both knew their father would never allow him to have a kitten — and they also knew why.

She recalled the last conversation she had with her father about it.

"It'll be good for him to take on some responsibility," she had pleaded. "It'll teach him how to love and care for something besides himself. What's so awful about that?"

"I don't want another pet," he'd said. "Not after what happened. And that's final."

Fran thought her father was ridiculous to blame Danny's drowning on the fact that he was trying to save their dog.

The dog had been a birthday gift for Fran.

The twin's parents had given Danny an Indian Scout motorcycle for his fifteenth birthday and Fran, a Boston Terrier puppy. The black and white pup was the runt of the litter and so tiny she would crawl into a pickle jar and fall asleep. Fran named her Pickles. That dog went everywhere with the twins. Nobody ever saw them without that dog.

The kitten gift would not go over well, and Fran was aware of that.

However, she was a flight test pilot. While other pilots flew within the 'envelope,' a rectangular limitation of safe speeds and safe altitudes, flight instructors trained Fran to fly outside of the envelope and push the limitations of flight. She also pushed the limits when she wasn't operating an aircraft, when necessary.

The Finkel's phone rang. Seamus ran down the hall and answered it before Fran could.

"It's John," Seamus said, handing her the phone.

Fran had been going steady with John Sorenson for almost three years. A clean-cut fellow with that nice boy-next-door look. Anything nice about him stopped there.

"John?" she said into the receiver.

"Fran, guess what?" John said. "I enlisted."

He'd passed his flight test last week. Fran knew he intended to enlist after that. Yet still, it surprised her. It seemed so sudden.

"Do you know where you'll be stationed or when you're leaving?" she asked.

"I don't know yet," he said, sounding annoyed. "I need to get trained first. After that, they'll decide where they can use me the most."

"Will you be here for the dance tomorrow?" she asked.

"Just tell her already!" someone shouted on John's line.

"All right, Ma!" he shouted back.

"Uh, yeah. Fran, the reason I'm calling is that well — since I'm leaving and all...I don't think we uh, we should see each other anymore."

She didn't understand how those words could cause the wave of pain that they did.

"You're breaking up with me?" she said, "over the phone?"

Seamus gasped. He was still standing next to her. She shook her head at him and rolled her eyes.

"Listen," John said, "it's for the best."

"Yes, I agree," Fran said coolly before hanging up.

Seamus was staring at her with sad puppy eyes.

"It's okay, little brother," she said, mussing his hair.

Fran went to her room, flopped on her bed, and stared up at the ceiling as tears rolled down her face. She didn't know why she was crying;

the breakup didn't devastate her, although it would have crushed her mother since she had assumed John would propose to Fran. Her parents were high school sweethearts, and that's what high school sweethearts do. Only Fran wasn't sure she wanted to be married — especially to someone as dreary as John.

He was self-centered and spoiled, but worst of all, he lacked passion. And Fran ached for love. He asked her to go steady when they were in high school. She tolerated John since there weren't any other boys that she cared to date. Not that any had asked her out. Boys typically found her more intimidating than attractive.

Fran knew his parents had often tried to convince him to break up with her. He told her they said she was too headstrong and not feminine enough for their son, but she knew they didn't like her because she worked on airplanes and was a "grease monkey."

As if one could view working in a fish cannery as a glamorous profession.

John's parents owned the seafood cannery in Newport Village. They told him he had to either work there or enlist in the military. To encourage him to get his pilot's certificate, they bought him a red and white Fairchild F-24 airplane that was easy to fly. One of the flight instructors who worked for Fran's father had trained John. He failed the written exam three times before he passed.

Fran dreaded the idea of being someone's wife, so she was also relieved. She recalled the conversation she had in the kitchen with her mother last year.

"Do you think you'd marry John if he asked you?" her mother questioned.

"I don't know," Fran said. "It's just that, well, I don't think I love him."

"Oh, Frances, you can learn to love him with time. You know it's just as easy to fall in love with a rich man as it is with a poor one." He was an only son and sure to inherit the family's thriving business.

"He's also quite boring," Fran said. "John never asks me anything. He only talks about himself."

"Pshaw child, that's what all men are like."

Her mother smiled at her and put down the rolling pin she was using to roll out dough. They were making biscuits; her mother always made enough to feed an army. Fran assumed she had the habit of making too much food because she'd learned how to cook at her family's restaurant.

"You can move to a big city after you get married, that'll be exciting enough. There'll be concerts, dancing and fancy restaurants."

Mrs. Finkel was a lover of the finer things in life.

"Life could be so splendid," she paused, "for you."

"Why did you marry Papa?" Fran asked.

Fran remembered the shadow that crossed her mother's face when she asked that.

"Because I was irresistible!" her father shouted from the living room where he was reading the paper. "She couldn't help herself!"

Her mother glared out at him from the kitchen and looked like she was about to answer him back, but she shook her head and remained silent.

Fran waited for her mother to answer her question.

Her mother sighed and brushed a wisp of hair out of her eyes. She always kept her hair tied up in a bun.

"Your father was charming," she said, smiling as she looked down. "And witty. He was also smart — is smart. And quite persistent. He asked me to marry him twice, and I told him no. When he returned from the war, he asked again. And well, that time, I said yes."

"Third time's a charm!" her father yelled out.

Fran chuckled.

Her mother lowered her voice. "But after we married, his family disowned him. You see, I'm not Jewish. Your father's family would not have recognized our children as Jewish. So, we moved far away. To here, Oregon."

"So...we're not Jewish?"

"You're half Jewish. Half Irish, half Jewish."

She pointed her finger at Fran. "You should always be proud of being either one and never listen to anyone who tells you otherwise."

Danny walked into the kitchen then. Tall and broad-shouldered, wearing coveralls. He'd been working in the hangar. Their mother lit up when she saw him. Fran noticed she always looked at him like he was a movie star.

"Wipe your boots, love," she said.

He grinned as he obliged her.

"Hey Fran, you know Doctor Gato's Stinson? Blew a tire landing just now."

Dr. Gato had been their family doctor for as long as Fran could remember.

"Oh, no!" Fran said, standing up. "Was he hurt?"

"Nah, he's fine. Can you help me fix it?"

"Your father can help you. Frances is busy," their mother said. "He's in the living room reading the paper."

"Papa!" Danny called out.

"Young man," their mother said, "we do not shout to each other in this home like some shanty Irish family. You walk in there and speak to your father like a proper gentleman."

Their mother considered "shanty Irish," poor and ignorant, while "lace-curtain Irish" were wealthy and educated. She preferred her children to behave as if they were lace-curtain Irish, although they were middle class.

CHAPTER 3

Fran had the same dream she had on many other nights. She was walking around an enormous plane riddled with bullet holes, trying to decide if it was flightworthy. She ran her hand along each of the wings, then climbed a ladder to check the propeller blades.

She stepped up onto one of the wings and dropped into the cockpit. Inside, she looked over the fuses and gauges on the front panel. Satisfied, Fran flipped the ignition switch. The propeller's blades came alive with a deafening roar as they began to turn. She realized someone was there beside her in the cockpit.

That's when she always woke up. Half-asleep, she sat up in bed and tried to make sense of her dream.

Danny had always spoken of flying big planes. *Was it Danny?* The young man in her dream didn't feel like her twin. And in her dream, Fran was in the pilot's seat. *But that was ridiculous.* The military didn't allow women to fly warplanes.

Her dream made no sense to her.

Early that summer, Fran went to the army's enlisting office, bringing logbooks in which she had recorded her piloting time. The recruiter told her women could not fly aircraft for the military. Fran didn't see why she couldn't be the first to do so, and she asked him to put her name on a list in case that rule changed. He told her there was no such list, thanked her for stopping by, and handed her back her logbooks without ever opening them.

Fran got up out of bed, dressed, and went into the kitchen to make breakfast for Seamus and her father. Her brother was out on his paper route, and her father was still sleeping. She baked a batch of cornbread muffins while a pot of coffee was percolating for her father. Fran looked out the window over the kitchen sink and saw Seamus walking towards the house in the morning light, carrying the newspapers he hadn't sold. He walked through the kitchen, then went to the fireplace and tossed the extra papers next to it.

"How did you do?" Fran asked.

"Not bad. Sold forty out of the fifty, made almost two dollars."

He sat down on one of the worn wooden chairs at the kitchen table. Fran placed the muffin pan down in front of him.

"Thanks," he said, grabbing at the fresh muffins. "I may go back in later to sell the other ones, see how it goes. Maybe you can drop me off in town after school today?"

Their father walked into the kitchen and poured himself a cup of coffee. He sat down next to Seamus.

"I see you put your newspapers next to the fireplace. Remember to empty the trash bins after you get home from school and burn any paper in them."

"Yes, sir."

"Son, after you're done with your chores in the house, I want you to help me out in the hangar. I have two planes that need to be checked out."

Fran placed a bowl of oatmeal in front of her father and took a seat at the table.

"I can help you, Papa," she said. She picked up a muffin and spread raspberry jam on it.

"What about the dance tonight in Newport?" her father asked. "I thought you'd be planning to go with John."

Fran took a bite of muffin and didn't answer him. She glared at Seamus, who wisely chose to keep quiet. She didn't feel like telling her father. He'd find out soon enough through the grapevine.

"John said he'll be leaving his plane with us now that he's enlisted," their father said, sipping his coffee. He picked up the newspaper beside him. "He wants to be a pilot in the army."

"John is the last person who should fly for the army," Fran replied. She suddenly understood why his phone call had upset her. It wasn't John she longed for.

"I want to be a pilot," Fran said.

"You already are a pilot and a darn good one to boot," her father said as he continued reading his newspaper. "What do you have, five hundred hours logged in?"

She had much more than that. Last month, when Fran turned 17, she had almost 2,500 hours.

"I want to fly military planes...for the army."

Seamus slapped his hands down on the table as he nearly choked on a mouthful of muffin. Fran ignored him.

"My child," her father said, reaching for the butter, "girls can't fly planes for the army, you know that."

"I can be the first."

"I don't think so. It's highly unlikely, that is."

"They will...I will. I already know it," she stammered, remembering her dream.

"Frances, they do not allow women to fly in the army. There are no female pilots in the Army Air Corps."

"What about Amelia Earhart?" Seamus asked.

"Papa, it's called the air force now," she said, correcting him. "They changed the name."

"Amelia Earhart was not a pilot in the *air force*," her father said.

"The guys at *The Oregonian* said reporters made Amelia up so they could sell newspapers," Seamus said. "She's pretty, plus she's a pilot, and people like to read about odd stuff like that."

"Seamus, that's one of the stupidest things I have ever heard," Fran said. "Of course, she is real — she flew over the Pacific!"

"Well then, where is she now?" Seamus asked.

"I don't know. Nobody knows. She's missing."

"Well then," their father added, "that's not making it look so good for women to fly for the army now, is it? Those planes cost a lot of money."

He put down his newspaper and pointed to an advertisement in the help wanted section.

"Frances, look here. They're hiring women to assemble aircraft at the Lockheed factory down in Burbank, California. You'd have an excellent chance at getting a job there. Why not fly down and see if they'll hire you?"

Fran rolled her eyes.

How am I going to make history as a famous pilot if I'm working in a factory?

"You think I should be a factory worker when I have ten times more flight time than any of the boys who are enlisting?"

They were quiet for a moment.

"I don't make the rules, Frances."

"It doesn't make a bit of sense to me." She dug her nails into the bottom of the chair.

"Me, neither," their father said. He went back to reading the newspaper.

"A girl being a pilot for the army," Seamus jeered. "That's the stupidest thing *I've* ever heard, *Frances.*"

Fran glared at her brother as she stood up and started clearing the dishes from the table.

CHAPTER 4

Fran woke the following morning to the sound of clanging pots and pans coming from the kitchen. Whenever her mother made breakfast, the aroma of baking biscuits would waft through the house as it made its way to her bedroom. Soon after, she would hear a familiar knock on her door.

"Frances," her mother would whisper. "It's time to get up."

She would climb out of bed and dress for school, unless it was the weekend. Then she would work in the hangar; in pleasant weather, she would even fly one of the planes. Those days she would dress quickly, hurrying to beat her twin brother out of the house.

But when Fran opened her eyes, the house was silent. Reality sank in. Mother had left four months ago, and they had not heard from her since. And there was no reason to rush to the hangar today. Danny would never be there again. Fran curled up in a ball as she felt the pang of the loss of her twin. It was like losing an arm and forgetting it was gone, having a ghost of the limb remaining in its place.

Her brother had resembled a young Ernest Hemingway, and like the famous writer, he planned to work as a news correspondent. Danny kept a journal and carried it with him everywhere. Fran recalled how he was always writing something down. Words no one would ever read.

It was Seamus who had broken the silence that morning. When he closed the front door, a hook on the kitchen wall gave way, causing the pan hanging on it to come crashing down onto the stove, startling Fran out of her slumber.

She looked out her bedroom window and thought about her younger brother riding his bike over the hills and into Newport's downtown section. At the waterfront, there were restaurants, pubs, shops and the cannery. He would pick up fifty copies of *The Oregonian,* their daily newspaper. Each day, fishermen dropped off newspapers they had picked up in Portland and left them on the loading docks as they continued trolling Yaquina Bay, pulling in their crab traps along the route, stopping at each of the tiny fishing villages along the coastline.

Most of the people who bought papers from Seamus were on his regular route, and like most Oregonians, they liked to talk. Unfortunately, Seamus was also a bit of a chatterbox. This combination made him late for school more often than not, something his father and the headmaster did not appreciate.

That morning the sky was a deep uniform gray. It'll be like this for the next few months, Fran thought as she watched the raindrops drizzling down the window. *Some days more rain than other days, but you can count on seeing some rain every day.*

Fran turned on her bedside lamp and looked down at the cocktail ring on the nightstand. Its large, red oval-shaped gemstone appeared to glow like a fire ember when the light hit it in a certain way. A little over a month ago, her father had given her the ring for her birthday. It had belonged to her mother. Fran wasn't one for wearing jewelry, but she treasured that ring.

Whenever the rains came, Fran's mother used to spend the day on the sofa listening to songs on the radio as she stared out the window. Fran would catch her crying when she thought nobody was looking. She wondered what her mother was crying about but didn't dare ask. *What if she didn't want to be a mother? Perhaps her life didn't turn out the way she had expected.*

Fran didn't want the weather to change her mood; she didn't want to be like her mother. She knew that one should never think negative thoughts because we become what we think.

At least that's what her book on positive thoughts said.

Her Uncle Conrad had left her that book when he and Aunt Elsa came out from New Orleans for Danny's memorial service earlier that year. Fran went over to her bookshelf and picked it up. She'd read it a few times over the summer and underlined some paragraphs. She opened the book and flipped to one of the highlighted sections. It was about refusing to think of what you don't want and only thinking of what you do want. It also said you must expect it, even when whatever is happening in your life is the opposite of what you want.

Something about the passage resonated with her. At that moment, she felt a mystical connection to those words.

Fran wondered if she could control her destiny with positive thoughts. She wasn't sure how it could work, but what if this was how she could find other female pilots or even be allowed to fly warplanes? Her parents would be so proud they'd never even mind that John had broken up with her — their daughter was a famous female pilot! They could brag about it and tell everyone how amazing she was, just like they used to when they spoke of Danny.

Impossible...or was it?

She read about how desire was an energy that emitted out of all living beings. It projected itself into the Universe. If that desire was strong enough, it could attract anything. This worked for anyone who believed in it.

But Fran wasn't convinced.

She sighed as she climbed out of bed. Fran dressed and then went to the kitchen. She changed the calendar hanging on the wall to November and started a pot of coffee for her father.

For his birthday, Fran made Seamus his favorite: a blackberry cobbler. His father gave him a watch. His disappointment was obvious to Fran, and her heart went out to him.

Later that morning, Fran drove her father's pickup truck down the coast to Depoe Bay. She stopped at a tiny shack across the street from the ocean where a sweet little old lady lived. She had met Fran a month ago and agreed to let her choose a kitten from her cat's new litter once they were old enough to be on their own. Fran already knew which one to pick for Seamus. She thanked the woman then placed the kitten in a box and drove her to her new home. Before going to the house, Fran smuggled the kitten into the hangar and hid her in the storage closet. She planned to surprise Seamus with his birthday present after dinner.

Fran returned home only to find her brother sulking on the sofa in the living room, staring out the window. She sat down beside him.

"She's not coming back, is she," he said, referring to their mother.

He was hoping she'd show up for his birthday, Fran thought.

"Maybe she will," Fran said, trying to sound optimistic. "Don't lose hope. She might surprise us one day. You never know."

As if saying it will make it happen. Impossible.

"Why don't we head out to the hangar and get that Staggerwing ready for Mr. Dunn?" their father said to the two siblings as he walked into the living room. "He flew his plane all the way over from Bend for its scheduled maintenance checkup. These planes are expensive, you know. We don't want to keep him waiting."

"Yes," Fran said sarcastically, "wealthy executives like Mr. Dunn who can afford a Staggerwing don't enjoy waiting."

Their father gave her a disapproving look.

Pilots flew from all over the Northwest to have their planes maintained by the Finkels. The shop's location was ideal. Pilots could see the coastal mountain range to its east; the Cascades, which included Mount Jefferson and Mount Hood, their peaks snowy even in July, to the north. The Pacific ocean was to the west. These landmarks made it easy for pilots to find the tiny airstrip nestled within the surrounding forest.

Fran looked out the bay window at the rain. It was growing dark earlier in the day. In the fall, the weather at the coast turned wild and unpredictable. It made her miss Danny. She sighed.

"Seamus, I'll take Mr. Dunn's plane for a test flight first thing in the morning after the weather clears. Why don't you help Papa finish up the maintenance check?"

The wind and rain whipped into the bushes against the front of the tiny house, making a considerable scraping noise.

"Fran," he countered, "you know you could finish the Staggerwing's maintenance check in half the time it'll take us."

She didn't answer him. She knew he was right.

"You two figure it out," their father said. He put on his coat and hat. "But I'll need at least one of you to come outside to hold the flashlight."

After he left, Seamus glared at Fran.

"See?" he said. "I knew it. No kitten!"

"Did you make up a picture in your mind?"

"Yes, I did."

When Seamus said he wanted a kitten for his birthday, Fran gave him specific instructions on how to receive what he wanted. It didn't matter if it was a can of corn or a kitten; he could have it if he imagined his wish with as many details as possible. Although he scoffed at the notion, this was how the thought book said it worked. And Fran needed to test that theory out on somebody, so she figured it might as well be her little brother.

"I imagined a fluffy one, a female," he had told her. "She has long hair and black on the tips of her ears, uh, and toes."

Fran smiled as she listened, barely able to keep herself from telling him. She already knew what he wanted since he talked about it so much; she had picked out the kitten that matched his imagined one as best as she could.

"Well, if you did all that thinking about the details, then it'll happen. The days not over yet." She winked at him and went back to washing the dishes. "Trust me."

He grunted in response and pulled a sweater over his head. Fran watched from the window as he trotted in the rain towards the airport to help their father. Once he was out of sight, she grabbed her raincoat and rushed outside. Then Fran stopped at the end of their driveway and went back inside. She turned all the knobs on the stove to the right, making sure each one was off.

As she ran to the hangar, she remembered what her father had said.

"Fran, I know, just like everyone else here on the Oregon Coast knows, that he wants a kitten for his birthday. But, I cannot understand why on earth a teenage boy would want such a thing. Why not a motorbike or new fishing gear or a canoe?"

What difference did it make? He could have whatever he wants if he believes he can. That's how it works.

As she ran down the road towards the hangar, she was full of pride. *He'll see, positive thinking works!*

Although Fran may have helped it along, she still considered this to be an official manifestation of a desire.

Her father was already working through the maintenance checklist with Seamus when she walked past them.

"Uh, I left my magazine in the office," she mumbled as she went into the hangar.

Fran turned on the lights. Sidestepping the aircraft in various stages of repair, she headed for the storage closet where she had stashed the kitten.

But she wasn't there.

Fran searched the hangar, looking under the planes. She peered out into the rain for any signs of the little feline. She could see her father walking around the Staggerwing, feeling along the side of the plane for any loose bolts. Fran knew he intended to check every item on his list, even in the pouring rain.

They were the only souls at Seal Rock Airport. She crept out of the hangar and tried to look casual as she walked alongside the building.

There wasn't enough room in the hangar for the massive Staggerwing, named because its lower wing was closer to the front of the aircraft. The upper wing was more set back, out of the pilot's view.

Seamus, now officially 15 years of age, stood underneath the plane's enormous propeller. The soaking rain had darkened his strawberry blond hair; his wet clothes clung to his body as he sullenly waited for his father to complete the plane's inspection. He stood in front of the aircraft, holding a flashlight so his father could see what he was doing as the daylight slipped into darkness.

"Isn't she magnificent?" their father said. Seamus shrugged.

Their father was meticulous in his efforts to ensure a plane was airworthy. He climbed onto a stepladder and lifted the metal cover that protects the engine. He felt around for any debris that might have blown inside. Seamus shined the flashlight into the compartment that held the engine and searched for fluid leaks.

Fran noticed her father had his ear turned toward the plane as if he was listening to something. He cocked his head to the right and pushed his cap back, furrowing his brow.

"Seamus," he said, stroking his beard. "There's something way down in the back behind the engine...but I don't know what it is."

When Fran heard that, she took a few steps towards them.

As they peered into the darkness of the plane's innards, they heard a faint meow. Seamus gasped and pulled away. His father shook his head and looked up at the heavens.

"Oy vey!" he cried.

Another tiny meow came from inside the plane's underbelly. Mr. Finkel reached his hand in as far as he could, but his attempts at wiggling his fingers to lure the kitten out made it crawl even deeper into the plane. They heard another meow, this one much fainter.

"It's scared," Seamus said.

Their father scowled. A downpour of rain began.

"Fran!" Seamus shouted. "There's a kitten stuck in the plane!"

Their father crouched down under the aircraft, and Seamus waved the flashlight up inside. They heard another tiny meow. Fran stepped up next to her brother.

"Can you hand me the flashlight?" she asked.

She climbed up the stepladder in front of the propeller. Aiming the flashlight with her right hand, she squeezed her left arm between the spokes and then waited. After several minutes, she felt a soft, furry warmth crawl into her palm. Fran gently pulled her arm out. It was the kitten, only now she looked more like a drowned rat.

Their father looked at his daughter and then at the kitten.

"Did you put that creature inside Mr. Dunn's plane?" he said accusingly.

"I most certainly did not," she answered.

"Then how'd it get in there?" he demanded.

Fran shrugged.

Their father shook his head. "I'm pretty sure you had something to do with it, young lady," he muttered.

She ignored him and gingerly handed the kitten over to her brother. Seamus had already pulled his sweater up and over his head, waiting to wrap her inside of it.

"That's great," their father said. "I guess now we have a cat."

"What are you going to name her?" Fran asked.

"How do you know she's a girl?" Seamus asked.

"I just know."

"Bernice. I want to name her Bernice."

"Papa, can I help you finish up the check?" Fran asked.

"Meh, it's too dark now. Gonna call it quits for the night. Maybe you can come out first thing in the morning with me?"

Fran was eager to take the Staggerwing for its test flight. The plane was gorgeous and could fly over 200 miles an hour. However, she looked up at the starless sky and decided it would stay grounded until visibility cleared.

"Sure. I'll take it for a test flight once this cloud cover blows off."

Fran walked home with her brother in silence as he carried his kitten. The rain had stopped for the moment. She considered bringing up how thinking got him what he wanted but didn't feel Seamus was mature enough to understand. She thought she would be wasting her time.

After they arrived home, they found leftover salmon and Dungeness crab for the kitten. Seamus poured some cream into a small saucer. He grinned when Bernice gobbled up the seafood and lapped at the milk, purring loudly. She was dry now, and they could see the little black pointed tips on her ears. Fran kissed Seamus goodnight, and he gently lifted the kitten and held her to his ear as he carried her to his bedroom, humming.

Fran recalled how her mother used to sing that tune around the house. She looked at the framed photo on her nightstand of her mother wearing a black evening gown and a long string of pearls. It was taken at a gala in New Orleans, years before Fran was born. A poster of movie star heartthrob Gregory Peck hung over Fran's bedroom door. She used to daydream about meeting him and dancing with him. Fran would drift off to sleep to that fantasy many a night. But now, when she had trouble falling asleep, she would allow the memories of her mother to soothe her.

Fran's mother had graduated from a private college in New York, where she majored in music and fine arts; she went on to become a classical pianist and champion ballroom dancer. When she moved to Oregon with her husband, the lack of sophistication was a bit of a shock for Mrs. Finkel. She called it a "cultural wasteland" and began teaching piano and dance lessons to the local children. When they were old enough, she insisted her three children learned to dance as well. Both boys hated dancing when they were younger but wanted to please their mother. With time they improved and enjoyed it much more. Fran didn't see the point in it, but she didn't mind it, either. Her mother would play the piano, and they always wound up laughing until she couldn't stand up. Fran had fond memories of those days. She liked to see her mother laughing, to see her happy.

The tune Seamus had sung continued to play in her head. She tried to remember the name of the song as she drifted off to sleep.

CHAPTER 5

After breakfast, Fran walked over to the hangar to work on one of the planes in the shop. When she went into the office, she glanced at the photo of Danny hanging on the wall. It was taken when he was five years old, perched atop a Lockheed Vega airplane. It was the same year her father opened his maintenance shop at Seal Rock Airport. Fran's mind traced back to the time of those early years in her life.

Joel Finkel had built the house they now lived in a mile away from the shop. Before moving, they lived in Yachats, a remote beach town on the Oregon Coast near U.S. Route 101. Yachats is rocky; when the tide goes out, beachcombers find an assortment of sea creatures left behind in the tide pools.

Fran's first memory was walking barefoot over the sharp barnacles that covered the beach rocks. The icy-cold Pacific water lapped at her ankles as she and Danny searched for starfish during low tide.

Terrified by the ocean, their mother would stay back on the shore, away from the water. She said it was full of vicious sea creatures lurking in the deep, waiting to bite them.

"Look out for sneaker waves!" she would shout to the twins over the ocean's roar. Sneaker waves were enormous random waves that rose out of the water without warning in October, November, April and March. They would sweep away unsuspecting victims who had dared turn their backs to the sea.

Aviation grew more popular over the next decade. Their father began to give flight lessons, and when he could find one, he hired the occasional instructor to help with training.

After moving to Seal Rock, the twins spent most of their youth at the hangar, fascinated by the stories told by visiting pilots.

As soon as he was old enough, Danny started working in the hangar. Since they were mostly inseparable, Fran spent her days helping around the hangar too, when she wasn't in school.

Whenever a plane would fly overhead, Danny would yell out to her, "What is it?"

"It's the Miller's Fairchild," Fran would answer.

"How do you know?"

"The engine whines when it banks left."

At a very early age, Fran could recognize what type of plane was flying overhead by the sound of its engine. She knew what make it was, sometimes even the model. She could identify several by their call sign, and if they'd ever been to the shop, she could tell you who owned the plane.

As she grew older, the number of planes and pilots in the air skyrocketed. Farmers used planes for crop dusting, and young men barnstormed with them, flying from town to town, landing in farm fields, and charging five dollars a flight. The wealthy used them for commuting and racing. Nearly every day, a new type of plane flew over Seal Rock Airport as aircraft engineering boomed.

Whenever a new model came to the shop for maintenance, their father showed Danny how to check it out and read the technical drawings. Fran watched over their shoulders. When Danny turned 10, the instructors took him out and taught him how to fly. Fran asked if she could learn, but their father said no. She begged the instructors to take her anyway and oftentimes they did. She was 11 when she soloed for the first time. Their father fired the flight instructor who let her fly alone, but he gave up trying to keep her on the ground after that.

The twins used makeshift wooden blocks to reach the plane's rudder pedals. Danny always let Fran fly when they went out together, and they kept track of their flight hours in their logbooks. As a result, Fran had more hours of flight time logged in by age 15 than most adult pilots.

Danny became certified as a mechanic first, even though Fran was the one with the mechanic's ear. She had a sixth sense of knowing when something was wrong. She was always listening as good pilots do. Her brother was not interested in the mechanics of a plane. Danny loved aerobatics. He was a freewheeling daredevil. Fran was his opposite. More level-headed than her twin, she had her own rules for flying with such stringent limitations that most pilots would consider her extreme.

Fran's twin wanted to be a fighter pilot, like their father. He planned to enlist as soon as he was old enough. Fran would remain silent as she listened to Danny tell her how he would first fly trainers, then pursuit planes and then bombers. After that, he would go overseas to help win the war against Hitler.

They had heard and read about what was happening to the Jews over in Europe. She recalled how Danny counted the days until he could join the military. He checked them off on his calendar while wondering if the United States would enter the war.

At the time, the country was divided over that decision.

People spoke of World War I as the war to end all wars. Some said America should assist the countries fighting Hitler. Others said the nation should prepare to defend itself if necessary.

Although Mr. Finkel had been a fighter pilot in World War I, he never spoke about it.

During the summer, the twins flew their Cub up and down the Oregon Coast, when weather permitted, taking turns as pilot in command. They even squeezed in a trip from time to time with Seamus. Sometimes, instead of flying to the coast, her brothers flew along the Willamette River. They would land, then build a campfire and spend the night. Other times Fran would fly with one of her brothers to a spot on the coast to watch the sunset. They'd make a fire and sleep on the beach.

Fran knew her mother didn't like it when they went out on these adventures, but as long as they kept up with their schoolwork and dance lessons, she allowed them to be wild and free. She had only tried to stop them once.

Unfortunately, they hadn't listened to her.

It was the last time Fran flew with her twin.

CHAPTER 6

On a rainy morning in late November, Fran and her father were reading the newspaper over breakfast when she noticed a section was missing.

"Papa, do you have the society page?" she asked.

He flipped through the pages. "No, young lady. I do not."

"Hmm, well, it's not in today's paper."

Seamus walked into the kitchen and dropped his extra papers on the table, then sat down.

"Seamus, our paper doesn't have the society section."

"Um, yeah," he said, glancing nervously over at her as she flipped through one of the extra papers. "It's not a big section in this issue."

"Oh, here it is," Fran said. "It must have been just our paper missing it."

"What a nice-looking couple," she said, glancing at the first page.

She turned to the next page and then stopped. Her mouth dropped open in shock.

"No, that's impossible." She turned back to the engagement section's first page. The photo was of John, her ex-boyfriend, his arm around a blonde, full-figured young woman. Fran couldn't believe what she read next:

Mr. and Mrs. Paul Crane of Boston, Massachusetts, announce the engagement of their daughter, Evelyn Jean, to John Sorenson III of Newport, Oregon.

The future bride, known as EJ, is a native of Seattle, Washington. Her father is an indoor plumbing supplies dealer.

She was presented to society at the International Debutante Ball in Seattle. The future prospective bridegroom is the son of John and Mary Sorenson. The bridegroom enlisted in the U.S. Army Air Force to attend pilot training. The couple met at a summer gala in Seattle. The engagement took place in Victoria, British Columbia.

They plan a 1942 wedding in Seattle.

"A debutante, no less," Fran said coolly.

"I didn't want you to see it," Seamus said, "so I took it out of our paper."

He must have been seeing her all summer. It's bad enough to break up with me over the phone, but this is insulting. And humiliating.

Their father leaned over to read the article, then sighed.

"Oh, dear," he said. "Well, I thought he was a bit of a schmo."

Fran threw the paper down in disgust.

"I can't believe he was sneaking around behind my back, dating her. What a waste of my time."

"Men!" she shouted as she left the house, slamming the door behind her.

Fran didn't want to marry John, but she didn't like the idea that he had chosen somebody else. Someone blonde and busty from a wealthy family. And the nerve! To cheat on her all that summer while she was busy taking care of her father and brother. She had been too busy to notice that he hadn't been around most of the time.

She screamed up at the sky in frustration as she walked down the road to the hangar.

When Fran arrived, she looked around at the planes. She needed to fly somewhere far away to escape. She couldn't take the Cub because the instructors needed it. She found Skeeter in the back of the shop, rebuilding the burned-up Stearman engine.

"Skeeter, how's that Stinson's maintenance coming along?"

"All done and ready for its test flight, Fran."

Doctor Gato had brought in his big, beautiful plane for its annual maintenance check. The 4,000-pound Gullwing Stinson Reliant had over a 40-foot wingspan. It was a giant compared to Fran's plane. Its 300-horsepower engine was a fuel hog, but she would have enough gas to fly over 400 miles without stopping to refuel. Fran walked around the plane, checking it over. She knew the doctor wasn't planning to pick it up until next week. Fran went to the back office and put on her flight suit and parachute. When she came out, her father and Seamus were in the hangar.

"Fran," her father said, "you shouldn't be flying when you're upset. You know better."

"Upset?" she replied. She took a sample of the plane's fuel and checked it for water. "About what? John? Please, we broke up weeks ago. I'm over him."

"I'll need fuel," she said to Skeeter. He stood up and walked towards her.

"You broke up with John?" Skeeter said, surprised.

"No, he dumped me."

"Why didn't you tell me?" her father asked.

"Meh, it slipped my mind."

"Can I come with you?" Seamus asked her.

"No," their father said. "You get going, or you'll be late for school."

"It's early," Fran said. "I could have him home by dinner."

"He can't miss school, Fran. You know how the headmaster is."

"Fine," Fran huffed. "I'll head to the east. It's drier and better weather than the coast."

"Skeeter, can you help me push the Stinson out of the hangar?"

After they topped off the plane's fuel, she forced a smile at her father and waved to him.

Doctor Gato's plane was powerful, but Fran had flown it before and knew how to handle it. She pushed the throttle forward and the engine roared. The plane lifted effortlessly off the runway. Weightlessness is the best feeling in the world, she thought, as the plane climbed into the sky.

The trees and road looked smaller now. Once in the sky, Fran felt as if she had left her problems on the ground below. John did not break her heart, but she felt betrayed. He took what little trust of people she had and made her feel foolish. She wanted to leave home and never return.

The skies were clear except for a few fluffy clouds; visibility was well over ten miles. Fran was looking out off of her left wing at the snow on Mt. Hood when she heard a roar. The sky grew dark above her, and she looked up, terrified. She couldn't believe what was flying overhead.

Fran counted fourteen of the biggest bomber planes she had ever seen. She couldn't tell if they were U.S. military or the enemy. She dropped the Stinson's altitude to 900 feet in case she needed to land. Fran didn't know what to do. Her mind raced. *What if this is an attack?*

What if it's the Germans? Should I turn back? What's the procedure for declaring this?

Fran watched the ships as they flew in formation in front of her. They were the most impressive aircraft she'd ever seen, and right then she knew she wanted to fly one more than she had ever wanted anything else in her entire life.

As Fran followed them, she saw they were heading north towards Pendleton, a small town in the state's remote desert area. Fran knew it had an airport. She recalled hearing a few months ago that the army had designated it for combat training.

If they're planning to attack Pendleton, that's a bit of overkill.

She looked on as the bombers landed one by one at the Pendleton Airport. Fran hardly recognized the airport with its longer and wider runways, along with the newly built hangars erected on both sides. She called into the airport's control tower on the plane's radio and asked for permission to land.

After she taxied the Stinson off the runway, Fran parked the aircraft near the hangars. She got out of the plane and walked towards the row of bomber planes. A young man wearing sunglasses climbed out of one and hopped down in front of her.

"That is the most incredible airplane I have ever seen," she said to him.

"Oh, my! Hey there," he said with a smile. "Why, thank you, young lady. This is a B-25 Mitchell. I flew it here from Dallas."

He pulled off his sunglasses. "Say, are you a pilot?" he asked as he looked behind her at the Stinson.

"Yes, I am. You and the others just flew right over me."

"Was that you?" he asked, unbuckling his parachute. "That's a beauty of a plane."

Fran nodded.

"Would you mind directing me to the person in charge here?" she asked.

He pointed to the buildings in the distance.

"Go down there and ask anyone you see for Colonel Von Lekker."

Fran walked towards the army base. When she arrived, she saw an older man working in a guard shack. He scowled at her.

"What are *you* doing here?" he snarled. Fran was taken aback by his tone.

"I'm looking for Colonel Von Lekker," she said.

"What for?" he asked suspiciously. "Does he know you're coming?"

"I doubt it. I'm a pilot and want to find out about the flying that's done here at the training center."

"Sign this," he said, shoving a clipboard out the shack's window. Fran signed her name on the sheet.

"Frances Finkel," he said, reading her name out loud. He stared down at her.

"Things you see when you don't have a gun." The grumpy guard pointed at the door of a nearby building. "Go in there. I'll let him know you're on your way."

Fran headed in that direction. She turned back and noticed the guard still scowling at her.

What's his problem?

Fran headed over towards the office door. When she walked in, she saw an officer sitting behind a desk, speaking on the phone. Fran waited for him to finish his call. He was a little man with a pinched face and a weak chin. Something about him reminded her of a weasel.

"And who do have we here?" the weasel asked. He gestured for her to have a seat.

"My name is Frances Finkel. I'm a pilot."

"Did you fly here?" he asked.

"Yes, I did. I followed the B-25s here."

"Did you now?" The colonel cocked his head to one side.

"I have over twenty-five hundred hours in flight time as well as commercial, multi-instrument and multi-engine ratings," Fran told him.

"Do you know anything about the B-25?" he asked.

She shook her head.

"The B-25 Mitchell is a twin-engine bomber plane produced in factories in Dallas and Kansas City. It can travel over a thousand miles and has a wingspan of seventy feet."

"I'd like you to consider training me to fly them."

He laughed.

"You must be joking," he said. "You're not serious, are you?"

"Yes, sir. I am quite serious."

"Do you have any idea how much a B-25 costs Uncle Sam?" he said. "Over one hundred thousand dollars. If you actually believe I would trust a plane like that to some Jew girl, you need to have your head examined."

The crudeness of his response shocked Fran. *What difference does it make if I'm Jewish?*

The colonel looked her up and down in disgust.

"I don't care how much flight time you have had or what ratings you have. I don't have time to babysit a girl."

Fran still couldn't believe someone was speaking to her that way.

"You got a lot of nerve," he sneered, "showing up here."

She stood up to leave.

"That's right," he said, "you get out of my office! And don't dare fly in my airspace again or I'll have my men shoot you down."

CHAPTER 7

During breakfast on the first Sunday in December, Fran told her father she was planning to fly to the coast.

Alone.

She hadn't flown to the ocean since her last flight with Danny. There was a long pause before her father responded.

"Fran, are you sure? The weather can be squirrelly this time of year."

"I'm sure."

On Sundays, they usually slept in, but this morning Fran had been awake since dawn. She had made a big breakfast for her father and Seamus, who would be home after finishing his Sunday paper route. She nibbled pensively on a piece of toast. Something wasn't sitting well with her since she woke. Perhaps it was a dream that was still on the edge of her conscious mind, but she couldn't reach it, couldn't remember details, as if a wave had washed it off from the shore of her memory but had left fragments of it behind in the sand. Sometimes, an event or a word or a sight would revive the dream, and the scene would surge back to life on a mighty wave, washing back ashore what it had erased. Even the tiniest details would appear in focus. She let her uneasiness be, for now. Besides, it was impossible to force a dream to come into consciousness.

Fran looked on the kitchen wall at her mother's embroidery of a dragonfly. She thought about the time she'd been at the coast a few years ago when migrating dragonflies filled the air. Danny was there, writing in his journal as usual, while she was sitting back, looking up at the sky. She told him they looked so precise, flying in formation.

"You would notice that. You're such a perfectionist," he had said, teasing her.

He called that day "Dragonfly Day" and declared they would celebrate it each year after that. Whenever she saw a dragonfly, she felt a tiny stab in her heart. It was the little details that cut the deepest.

"Even after we're grown up and old and wrinkled," he proclaimed, "we'll be sitting in our rocking chairs, watching the dragonflies through our spectacles." Fran smiled at the memory and winced.

It was one of those days. She needed to escape, to fly into the sky as far away as she could.

She noticed the clock on the wall. It was after nine. Seamus wasn't home yet from delivering his papers.

"Seamus is late," she said to her father.

He sighed. "Should we go look for him?"

She thought about it for a minute and said it didn't seem necessary, not yet. It wasn't Seamus on her mind.

Fran was restless.

She packed a sleeping bag, a tent, a can of beans and some dry firewood — in case the wood at the coast was too wet to burn. She planned to build a fire on the beach and watch the ocean. She would spend the night if the weather turned bad. Of course, her father would worry if she stayed overnight, but he also knew she would make the safest choice.

Fran waited for the morning fog to burn off before leaving. Then, she flew the Cub up into the clearing skies, turning out west at a 270-degree heading. Once she saw the ocean on her horizon, she flew along the coastline. Fran searched for the flat strip that she and her twin brother used as a landing spot.

It was breezy on the beach. After climbing out of the plane, Fran tied the Cub down and positioned it so that a gust of wind couldn't flip it over. She walked to the water's edge and looked out at the ocean. The waves pounded against the rocks as the sea foam flitted across the shoreline.

She tried to block out the events of that day — the day of the accident — yet the memories rushed into her mind without mercy.

It had been the first day of good flying weather. It was also a Sunday.

By then, it seemed the rains had gone on forever. It felt like an eternity since the twins had last gone flying. They both passed their pilot exam on their sixteenth birthday, right before the weather turned bad, and they were itching to be up in the sky after a long, wet winter.

The sky was cloudless and a magnificent color blue. The twins wanted to look for the harbor seals. One could typically find them a bit further south in either Yachats or Waldport. Fran figured the seals would be out, what with all the recent rain. There would be hundreds of them basking in the sunshine along the beach.

Their father was in the hangar working on a plane that morning. Fran asked if they could take the Cub to the coastline. He went outside and looked up at the sky.

"Sure," he'd said. "Just be back for dinner. Weather could come in quick, and I want you both here for school tomorrow morning."

The twins dragged the plane out of the hangar and began to go over the checklist. Fran wanted to go through the entire list since they hadn't flown the Cub in months.

"The day is practically over, Fran," Danny had whined. "Can we just go already?"

"We need more fuel," she had told him.

"Nah, we got plenty!" he had disagreed.

They didn't. They had just enough. If anything went wrong, the twins wouldn't have enough to make it back. Fran filled the plane's fuel, which made Danny that much more annoyed. Pickles jumped up into the front seat. Fran told her no, but Danny wanted to take the dog with them.

"She'll scare the seals," she had argued. They started bickering, and that's when their mother came over.

Fran thought it was strange for her to come to the hangar; she rarely did. She didn't like all the noise: the drilling and hammering, engines revving, propellers whirling.

"Where do you two think you're going?" she had asked. Danny told her they were going to look for seals.

"Oh, I don't know about that. I have a bad feeling about it. I don't want you going."

"Ma, look at this weather!" Danny said. "I don't know how we can pass it up. It's Oregon! We need to enjoy the sunshine when it's here."

"Papa said it was okay," Fran had shot back at her.

Their father came over when he heard that comment.

"For crying out loud, Margaret," he said, "just let them go."

Their mother walked away out of earshot, their father following. The twins watched and waited to see who would win as their parents discussed the matter. Their mother kept shaking her head as he tried to convince her to change her mind.

"Ma!" Danny had shouted. "I promise you with all my heart we'll be careful. What if we only go to Yachats, and if we don't see the seals, we come home? That's only a twenty-minute flight. We can be back here in an hour. You can drive to the coast and watch us."

Fran wasn't sure how he did it, but he convinced her to let them go that day.

Mothers always have a favorite, even if they won't admit it. Fran knew it wasn't her — that was pretty obvious. It was Danny. She loved him with all the love there is.

The twins agreed Danny would pilot out and Fran would fly the return flight. Danny hopped into the Cub, pushed in the choke and turned the ignition key. Fran grabbed one of the propeller blades and swung it down. The propeller began spinning. Fran climbed into the cockpit and waved to their parents. Their father waved back, but their mother turned around and walked towards the house.

They were airborne and over the coast in a matter of minutes. It was a glorious day, and the ocean sparkled as if it was full of diamonds. The seals were out just a little north of Yachats, near where the Finkels used to live. They saw dozens of new seal pups with their mammas. There were big ones and small ones, some spotted, some tan, some gray. Their round eyes reminded Fran of dogs.

Danny landed in their usual spot. She remembered what he was wearing: sunglasses, a pair of old jeans and a navy knit sweater with a t-shirt underneath. They knew to dress in layers; it grew cold at the coast when the sun hid behind a cloud. Fran was wearing a pair of khaki pants, an oversized sweatshirt, and a baseball cap to avoid sunburn. She laughed at something funny that her twin said. She wished she could remember what that was.

He ran off towards the seals, and Pickles followed. The little dog sped past him as they headed toward the ocean's edge. He didn't want to spook the seals, but Pickles raced him to the water. Danny was trotting along at a slower pace, soaking up the sunshine and ocean breeze. He stopped and turned to wave at Fran, his back to the sea.

She was one hundred yards away from the shore when she saw it. The wave was at least 60 feet, almost twice as high as their house. Danny saw the terror in her face and read her mind.

They both knew about sneaker waves.

But to her horror, he spun around and ran as fast as he could, right towards the wave. He picked up their dog and clung to her as the wave came. Fran didn't remember what happened after that. She wanted to scream, but nothing came out. She tried to run, but her legs wouldn't move.

Fran remembered later, after the wave, looking up at strangers on the beach. Someone must have called the police because two officers were standing over her.

"Are you okay, miss?" one asked her. "Can you hear me?"

She was a little blurry-eyed but nodded. They asked her who she was, and she told them.

Fran remembered climbing out of the sheriff's car in front of their house. She would never forget her mother's face as she stood on the front steps, watching her daughter walk towards the house, her clothes and hair still dripping with water; that sickening look of utter despair as she gazed beyond Fran, waiting for Danny to come out of the police car.

Mrs. Finkel left a few months after the accident. Fran woke up early that morning and watched from her bedroom window as she climbed into a taxi. Her mother never wrote or called after that. Fran assumed she'd returned to New Orleans, her hometown.

"She blames me for what happened!" she screamed at the ocean. "If you were still around, she'd still be here! Was it worth it? The sacrifice? To throw away your life?"

Fran knew the answer.

He'd do it a million times over again if he had to.

She felt the ocean spray on her face as warm tears streamed down her cheeks.

Fran didn't understand *why* someone would do such a thing. She didn't believe she would have. And she didn't want to say that out loud because she was ashamed of herself.

On bad days Fran wondered what would have happened if they didn't get more fuel or if she hadn't been so nitpicky about the checklist. The "what if" thoughts overwhelmed her almost as much as the rogue wave that killed her brother and Pickles.

Fran ran along the shore until she was of breath. She was still warm from bitter anger when a cold chill shot up her spine.

Something was wrong. Fran felt an urge to go home and ran back to her plane. After she climbed into the cockpit, she looked out towards the sea.

"I'm sorry, Danny. I am not going to fly back here again. I can't. It doesn't mean I won't still think of you every second of every day."

After she was back in the air and soaring over the ocean, Fran could see gray Coast Guard planes out in the distance. She banked the plane and turned to head back home.

After landing at Seal Rock Airport, her father came out to meet her with a grim look on his face.

"Seamus hasn't come home yet," he said.

Fran ran to the Scout and jumped on the bike's seat. Its motor roared to life on her first kick. She sped down the road and turned onto Highway 101. With the ocean in her view, she scanned ahead for her little brother. She leaned into the bike at each turn, dreading to find him hurt. Or worse.

"Please," she prayed. "I can't lose him, too."

When she finally saw Seamus along the side of the road, she breathed a sigh of relief. He was walking with his head down, appearing deep in thought.

"Hey! Where's your bike?" she shouted as she pulled up alongside him. Fran rolled back on the throttle.

"Got a flat, so I left it at the docks," he said. "I gotta go back in later, anyway. Figured I could grab a patch kit at home to fix it."

"Why do you have to go back?" she asked.

"The news guys said they were printing an extra for later today."

He paused for a moment.

"Fran, they said the Japanese bombed a navy base in Hawaii this morning and killed a lot of people, civilians even, and destroyed battleships. It was pretty bad."

She shook her head. "That's horrible!"

"Do you think they'll attack the coast — here, where we are?"

"I don't know. We should go home and listen to the radio."

Seamus climbed on the back of the motorcycle behind her. They rode home in silence, both looking fearfully at their ocean as the Coast Guard planes roared out in the distance, across the horizon.

CHAPTER 8

During the attack on Pearl Harbor, the Japanese sank 18 American ships and killed 2,335 U.S. soldiers.

The next day, President Roosevelt announced the country would join the Allies in the war effort.

Most of the nation's qualified pilots began training to fly fighter planes. Soon after that, they left to fight overseas. Many female pilots with commercial licenses signed contracts with the government to teach young men how to fly. Once the students passed their flight test, they could enter training programs at army bases across the country.

After the barnstormers and the crop dusters in Oregon enlisted, they left their planes at Seal Rock Airport. The Finkels promised to watch over them until they returned. Most of the maintenance work at the hangar had stopped. To make matters worse, they banned all civil aircraft flights. They lifted the ban two days later, but the ban remained for the west coast. They didn't allow cars to use headlights either, making it impossible to see along the winding coastal highway that hugged the cliffs. During that time of year, fog forced people to avoid driving.

After four months of Oregon rains and nothing to do, Fran grew fidgety. She missed being in the air. She decided to fly east, over to the McKenzie River and then south, towards the state's warmer and drier areas. Fran was itching to brush up on stunt flying and decided to use one of the planes the boys had left behind.

She chose a Curtiss JN-4, also known as a "Jenny." The plane was perfect for performing aerobatics — Danny's favorite sort of flying. She remembered what happened the last time they flew together in a Jenny when following the McKenzie River.

"You have the controls," Danny had said.

"I have the controls," she said back to him. They made this exchange whenever they switched who was flying the plane. Danny unbuckled his seatbelt and climbed out of the cockpit. He made his way to the middle of the wing as the wind swirled in his hair.

"That's not funny!" Fran had yelled. "Get back in here! You're gonna get yourself killed!"

She and Seamus had made a tuna casserole that would last the few days she planned to be away. During the maintenance shop's downtime, she had been teaching her little brother to cook. She figured someone would need to know how to after she left. And she knew she would still be going, even though she didn't know when or how. Fran reasoned that if her mother did it, it must be possible. However, she wasn't sure if she could live with the guilt.

Fran packed a sleeping bag, two hard-boiled eggs, a flour sack full of fresh rolls she had baked that morning and a potato she could roast on the fire. She also brought two canisters of water.

The weather report for eastern Oregon sounded glorious, and Fran looked forward to spending a few days away to clear her mind.

As she went further away from home, she realized she had spent most of her time flying to the coast. The recent ban on flights allowed her to see the rest of Oregon. And there was so much to see.

She remembered reading a passage in the thought book that said if you say to yourself that you believe you'll do something, it will help you achieve it.

"I believe one day I'll fly planes that can travel across the entire country," she announced to herself.

But for now, Fran headed to the Klamath region, over towards Crater Lake. The lake had formed when a volcano erupted thousands of years ago. It left a 5-mile wide, 2,000-foot hole on top of Mount Mazama. Several hundred years of rainfall filled the bowl up with rainwater. It was the bluest color on the planet. The Klamath tribe were living there when it happened, and they still inhabited most of that area.

As Fran was flying over the Klamath reservation, she remembered her mother saying they believed the souls of good people lived on the lake, but evil souls dwelled on the bottom. Sometimes tribe members gathered on the shore to commune with the dead. The brave ones dove in late at night and swam to its depths. Fran shuddered at the thought.

When she arrived at the lake, she started practicing stunts. While she was rolling the plane into loops and spins, she noticed a boat out on the lake. The people in it waved to her, and she tipped one of the Jenny's wings to wave back.

After she had practiced enough, Fran found a flat spot and landed. It was late in the day, so she gathered branches to build a fire. After the fire was roaring and she had finished eating dinner, Fran leaned back and looked up at the dark, moonless sky. She saw several shooting stars blaze overhead before drifting off to sleep.

The next morning, Fran hiked off from her campsite and headed towards Crater Lake's National Park. She climbed up the narrow, rocky path that led to a spot where she could see the entire lake. From there, she spied a group of Native Americans down below at the shore. They were taking a boat out on the lake.

"Hello, there," a voice from behind her said. Startled, Fran lost her balance and fell on the trail.

It was one of the Klamath tribe members. He appeared to be in his twenties, wearing jeans and a vest with colorful beads sewn onto it.

"I'm sorry," he said. "I didn't mean to frighten you, ma'am."

Fran stood up and composed herself.

"Were you the one flying the airplane over the lake yesterday?" he asked.

"Yes, sir," she said.

Fran noticed an older man, wearing a long headdress of feathers, trudging up the trail. His pants and shirt were buckskin, and he had moccasins on his feet. His face was worn with wrinkles, but his eyes glowed with youth.

"That's our chief," the younger Native American said. "I'm Dave. Dave Red Eagle."

"I'm Frances. Frances Finkel."

"Aren't you afraid to be out here, all alone?" he asked.

"No," she answered.

"Why not? Don't you know the lake is full of spirits?"

"Good spirits or evil spirits?" she asked.

"It depends on the observer," he said with a wink. "Can you show us your airplane? The chief has never seen one up close."

"Of course," she said. They strolled down the path towards the plane, slowing down so the chief could keep up with them.

"Do you know the meaning of your name?" Dave asked.

"I was told it means 'free one.'"

As they approached the plane, Fran could see a little girl standing by, admiring it.

"That's my daughter," Dave said.

"Meadowlark," he said to the girl, "you stay away now. It's dangerous."

The girl stared at Fran in awe.

"Do you fly it?" she asked.

Fran smiled at her. "Why, yes. Yes, I do."

"But you're a girl."

"Girls can fly planes, same as boys." Fran bent down to whisper in her ear. "And sometimes even better than boys."

The little girl giggled as the men kept a respectful distance from the aircraft.

"We have another favor to ask of you," Dave said. "The chief — he does not speak English, but he wants to see the omini birds one last time before he goes on to his next life."

"Sorry. What kind of birds?" Fran asked.

"Omini. The white people call them passenger pigeons. Legend has it they once flew in flocks of billions. They would blot out the sky for days. They like huge lakes — the birds do. The dragon in our lake protects the birds from evil men who want to hunt them. The white man killed off most of them, you see. This flock hides in the forest over by the

Lost River. People can't get into the forest. It's too densely wooded. It's safe for the birds. That way, they're protected from hunters."

"How far is it?" Fran asked.

"Around twenty miles east."

She thought about it. "The problem is, there are only two seats. I'll need to communicate with the chief, and he doesn't speak English."

Fran looked down at Meadowlark.

"Can she translate for him?" Fran asked. "She's small enough to squeeze in the back seat with me. The chief can sit in front."

Dave looked over at his daughter.

"Do you want to go?" he asked her.

She clapped her hands together.

"Yes!" Meadowlark exclaimed.

Dave said something in Klamath to the chief. He smiled at Fran and nodded his head to thank her.

Once Fran had completed a brief check of the plane, they climbed into the aircraft. Before taking off, she showed them how the mike worked so the chief could communicate with her via Dave's daughter. Dave translated the instructions, and the elder nodded to Fran. She gave their leader a thumbs-up. He gave her a thumbs-up back.

As they flew up into the sky, Fran couldn't help smiling at the youngster's squeals of delight and peals of laughter. Fran felt the same whenever she became airborne.

While heading to the east, Fran spotted a river below them. The chief spoke into the mike, and Meadowlark translated for Fran.

"That's Lost River," she said. "Follow it. It will bring you to the pigeon's forest."

After about fifteen minutes, Fran could see the forest below them. As she flew over the trees, a flock of birds rose into the air below the plane. Fran didn't want a bird to fly into the propeller, so she searched for a place to land, but the forest was too dense. As the flock grew, Fran climbed to a higher altitude. The birds remained at a low height but kept up with her at a speed of 65 miles an hour.

Wow, these birds fly fast.

"Can you ask the chief if he wants to go back now?" Fran said.

Meadowlark spoke into the mike. When the chief turned around, he was smiling. Fran could see tears rolling down his cheeks. He nodded at her.

"The chief said thank you. He can go now."

After they returned, Fran lifted the little girl out of the plane and then assisted the chief. He looked at Fran and said something she didn't understand.

"He said he has money to pay you for the plane ride," Meadowlark said. "Or he will say a prayer for you to find what you are seeking."

Fran smiled and nodded at him.

"I sure would appreciate that prayer. Please tell the chief I said thank you and that it was my pleasure."

Fran spent the rest of her day walking the trail around the lake, eventually venturing down to the water's edge. She enjoyed being near a shore again, even if it wasn't the ocean.

That night Fran heard the throaty calls of ravens in the trees above her camp. She remembered a Celtic folktale her mother had told her about the raven. It was known in Irish legends as the Morrigan, a shape-shifter. Guardians of the dead and transporters between life and death, they had magical powers.

The following day, Fran packed up and began to go through the plane's checklist to prepare for the flight back home.

Satisfied with everything, she started the plane. As she taxied away from her camp, the engine sputtered and stopped. Fran hopped out to investigate. She carefully rechecked the fuel for any signs of condensation. Then, she lifted the engine cover and looked around for any debris that may have blown inside.

Suddenly, she heard a strange cry. When Fran turned, she saw two ravens on the ground. They were closing in on a bird with striking colors. She watched as one of the ravens yanked a bright blue feather from the bird's tail. The bird made the same peculiar sound.

Those ravens are planning to kill that bird.

Fran walked towards the fight, and the bullies flew off into the trees. She crouched down close to the victim and lowered her hand. To her surprise, the bird climbed onto her finger.

"How odd! Why you aren't even afraid of me in the least."

Fran held the bird close and could see the ravens had pecked its head. She gently stroked the bird, then took the empty flour sack from the plane's cockpit and carefully placed the bird inside. She reached into the plane to turn the ignition key, then pushed down on the propeller's blade. The engine roared to life. Fran climbed into the cockpit and taxied for a bit, making sure the engine didn't sputter again before taking off into the morning air.

During the flight, the bird continued to make unusual noises. Fran didn't know what kind of bird it was but guessed it was a pigeon, probably one of the passenger pigeons she'd seen yesterday at the Lost River.

"Papa isn't going to like this, you know," she said to the bird.

When she arrived at Seal Rock Airport, Seamus was standing outside the hangar, waving her over. He ran towards her as she cut the engine.

"Happy Easter and Passover!" he exclaimed. The bird squawked a loud response.

"Oh, shoot," she said, "I completely forgot about Passover and Easter, too."

The Finkels generally overlooked religious holidays.

"What's in there?" he said, pointing at the moving bag.

"A bird."

Fran took the sack out of the plane to show Seamus. He peeked inside.

"Wow, he's a beauty!"

"He's injured. Ravens were attacking him. I'm going to keep him until he's better."

"Papa's not gonna like that. Are you going to name him?"

She thought about it for a minute. They didn't know if the bird was male or female.

"How about Easter?" she suggested wryly.

Seamus made a face and rolled his eyes.

"Papa is going to hate that name."

"Well, I'm not going to name the bird Passover," she said.

CHAPTER 9

Seamus was right. It did not please their father to have another pet. But Fran promised him it was only until the bird recovered from its injuries. It was a trusting bird and grew very fond of her as she nursed it back to health. Fran built a small cage of wood with one side made of mesh, allowing it to see out. Although she convinced her father that she would let Easter go after the bird had healed, Fran had other plans.

First, she went to Newport's public library and read whatever she could find out about pigeons. She learned she could teach them to carry messages back to a particular spot they considered home. Fran also learned that pigeons were being used in the war to deliver messages.

Only one field guide mentioned passenger pigeons, reporting the species as believed to be extinct. Fran assumed the birds had migrated to Oregon and remained there. There was a photo of a passenger pigeon in the guide and from the markings, she determined Easter to be a male.

After completely recovering from his injury, Fran decided she would try to train Easter to deliver messages.

She started by letting Easter free at the hangar and watched as the bird flew straight to their house. After doing that for several days, she made a cloth satchel to carry Easter in.

Fran put Easter into the pouch, strapped it across her chest, and rode Danny's motorbike a few miles away from the house. She stopped to place a small cylinder on Easter's leg with a note inside, then let the bird fly away. He was off like a shot. She could keep up for a while as she watched the speedometer climb to 40 MPH, 50 MPH, 60 MPH. Whenever Fran looked up, Easter was in the lead, but she didn't dare ride any faster. When she arrived at the house, he was already there, perched on the kitchen windowsill.

The training continued for weeks. Each time, Fran brought the pigeon further away, sometimes in miserable weather. But even in fog and rain, he always returned home before she did.

One day Fran took Easter up in the Cub, landed 50 miles away from their house, and then released him. The pigeon still made it home before she did.

On their next trip, Fran flew out to Corvallis in John's Fairchild, where she landed for fuel and then headed south to Grants Pass. The plane had a 145-horsepower engine and could cruise at speeds up to 125 miles per hour.

After flying 200 miles away from home, Fran landed and set Easter free. Once she arrived back at the Finkel's hangar, she rushed to the house to see if Easter was there yet. Seamus met her before she was halfway home.

"He's not here," he said. It was the first time Fran returned before the bird.

They both walked back together to wait for Easter to show up. An hour passed, and the pigeon still hadn't arrived.

"Do you think he got lost?" Seamus asked.

"I don't know," she said. "Maybe he just doesn't like to fly at night. Owls are out hunting."

Fran searched the sky and listened for any cries from birds of prey. Finally, far out in the fading light of the sunset, they could see the silhouette of a single bird flying towards their house.

"Amazing," their father said as he came up behind them. They all watched as Easter landed on Fran's bedroom windowsill.

After that, whenever she took an airplane or Danny's motorbike on a trip, Fran took Easter with her. And she always sent the pigeon home with a message for her father, letting him know she was safe. With that, he decided that the newest addition could stay.

CHAPTER 10

One morning in early summer, Fran's father announced over breakfast that he had a business idea.

"What if we start up a pilot training program with room and board?" he said. "Frances, you and I can be the instructors. Nobody's stopping pilots from flying over to Corvallis and east of that. We can even fly to Bend if we wanted."

"We can advertise it in the newspaper," Seamus offered.

Shortly after he placed an ad in the paper, young men began signing up for the Finkel's Flight School. Soon there was a waiting list because of the demand for training.

Future fighter pilots took flight lessons with the Finkels until they earned a pilot rating. After that, they trained with the military to fly warplanes. Each student left Seal Rock after completing sixty-five hours of primary flight time, the minimum hours required for a pilot certificate.

Lessons cost three hundred dollars and included room and board. When the weather turned foul, and they couldn't fly, students received ground school lessons. Frances and her father trained students to read flight charts and maps and communicate by radio to other pilots and air traffic control towers. The students learned how to create a flight plan and navigate by looking for landmarks such as roads, barns, railroad tracks, large rocks or rivers.

The Finkels turned the hangar's office into a boarding house for the student pilots. They installed four bunk beds and completed the training program as quickly as possible in order to instruct the next ones on the waiting list.

The young men were also well-fed. Fran woke up at four o'clock every morning to make meals for the day: breakfast, bagged lunches and dinners. Seamus was helping in the kitchen and becoming a decent cook. After everyone had breakfast, Fran and her father gave flight lessons until dark or until everyone came in for dinner. After dinner, she and Seamus would get a start on breakfast rolls for the following day.

One night while washing dishes, Fran commented on the students lingering outside of the kitchen window.

"Seamus, why are they out there? Don't they have something better to do — like study for their pilot exam?"

"Uh, because they *like* you," her little brother answered, his hands full of dough and flour. "You got mom's good looks," he continued as he rolled out the dough.

Fran sighed and shook her head. Although she had the same hair and eye color as their mother, she lacked her petite mouth and turned-up nose. There wasn't anything dainty about Fran, she was more handsome than she was pretty. But it wasn't her appearance that drew the boys, it was something else — something they didn't see in most other girls. It was her confidence.

Yet the boys treated Fran like one of them, and so it was all a mystery to her. She did not have girlfriends in school and didn't know what she would have talked about with them if she did. The girls were very interested in boys, and since Fran spent most of her time with boys, there didn't seem to be anything to discuss regarding that subject.

The flight school was going along like gangbusters until the Finkels ran into a problem. The students mastered how to take off, fly in the airport's pattern and land. However, before they could earn their pilot rating, they would need to fly alone from one airport to another, and the student pilots kept getting lost on these flights. It wasn't easy to learn how to recognize a particular barn or what a runway looked like from above. For them, all the towns and fields looked the same. The mind needs time to learn these things, but these boys — and a world at war — had little time to spare.

To assist the student pilots, Fran and Seamus flew over the areas where the students traveled on cross-country flights, noting any odd barn or other structure that could be a potential landmark. They brought cans of paint and ladders with them in their father's pickup truck and asked farmers if they could paint the coordinates and the name of the town on the tops of their barns. If a student pilot became disoriented, he could then have some idea of where he was. Over the summer, when Fran wasn't in a plane with a student, she and her little brother were climbing up onto barn roofs.

One day while out searching for landmarks, they discovered thousands of acres of sugar beet farms. They couldn't find a barn, but they saw a large tent and an extended trailer. Curious, Fran found a spot to land and investigate.

As she and her brother headed towards the tent, they saw a large man with a scraggly beard, wearing a straw hat. He waved them over as they came closer.

"Hello!" he shouted. "Please come in from the heat and sit!"

Something about the workers seemed odd to Fran as they walked across the field. Then she realized what it was.

All the workers were Asian.

Seamus grabbed her arm.

"Fran, look!" he said, "That's Doctor Gato — over there, bent over."

They stared in astonishment at the sight of their family doctor picking beets in the field.

"What brings you two youngsters out here?" the bearded man asked. "You lost?"

"We're looking for barns to paint locations on, sir," Fran said, "so that our student pilots don't get lost."

"Well, I'd rather not have you paint anything here if that's all the same to you. This here is what's called an internment camp, you see. For the Japanese. Figured we'd also need these sugar beets harvested and may as well put them to work."

"Did you capture them?" Seamus asked. "Are they enemies?"

The man scraped the dirt off of his boots onto the tent's floor.

"Well, not really. You see, boy, these are all the Japanese living in Oregon. We had to incarcerate them — government orders."

As Fran and Seamus left the area, they stared at Doctor Gato in disbelief. He was crouched over, his shirt soaked through with sweat. He didn't look up as they walked by. Fran didn't say anything to him, either. She knew it would have been too humiliating for him to be recognized.

CHAPTER 11

One late summer evening, as they were eating dinner with the students, Fran's father made another announcement. It seemed Mr. Finkel liked to save any important information of the day for mealtimes.

"I got a telegram today from the War Department."

Everyone at the table stopped eating to listen to what Mr. Finkel had to say.

"The government wants me to train student pilots," he said, "like we've been doing, but now the government will pay us, and then the boys won't have to. Fran, it seems your Cub is the perfect trainer for them to learn in before they're out flying the big planes."

Fran groaned. She felt the students were not getting enough flight training hours before going into the fighter pilot training program. Many had been sent overseas with only 200 hours of flight time. It wasn't enough training to know what to do if they had an emergency in a trainer — let alone what to do in a new fighter plane. And now, her father was going to become a part of the government's training process.

"They asked me to sign a one-year contract. Isn't that terrific news?" her father said. "They'll be sending you a telegram soon, Frances. I'm sure of it."

She didn't answer him and stood up to leave instead.

"Frances, did you hear what I said?"

She sighed.

"Papa, it's wrong. That's not enough time to hand them off to learn to fly military aircraft. You know, big planes."

"I know, but I don't make the rules."

"What if I signed a contract to be an instructor and they decide to let women pilots in the military? I won't be able to go then."

"That's not something to waste your life wishing for," he said, shaking his head. "Why do you want to be a military pilot? It's not a safe place for a young girl."

"Are you saying that if the government were to allow women pilots, you wouldn't let me join?"

"You would just leave us here alone, your father and your only living brother?"

"Fran, please don't go," Seamus pleaded. "Who would take care of us?"

She stood and walked outside without answering them. Then Fran marched back into the kitchen.

"Would it be okay for me to be a pilot in the army if Ma were still here?" she asked. "Is that why I need to stay?"

"Frances, it's too dangerous!" her father said, slamming his fist down on the table. "You could be killed."

"You wouldn't be saying that if I were a boy, you wouldn't be saying that to..." she stopped.

"Danny? Is that why you want to do this? For Danny?"

Fran contemplated his question.

"Maybe that's a part of the reason," she replied, "but it's not all of it. I feel like it's not right to keep women out of this war. And I don't know why. Maybe one day, I'll know why I feel so compelled about this. But I can't answer that right now. I just need to find out for myself."

Her father sighed.

"If you decide to go, that's your decision. You are an adult. But it is something I would forbid you to do."

Fran felt torn. Her father was always holding her back, and she resented him for it. He was definitely not interested in seeing her test her wings. In fact, he had the opposite plan for her. How could she reach for the stars while she was around him? And now, if she left and failed, she could never come back home. He'd never let her live it down. She would have to succeed. Then he'd change his mind. He would even be proud of her. Maybe her mother would be, too. It was possible, Fran thought. She imagined her mother at tea, bragging to the other ladies about her daughter, the military pilot. Fran laughed out loud at the thought.

Over the next few days, the tension in the Finkel household grew.

Seamus lightened up the mood by throwing a going away party for Skeeter, who had enlisted. The party was also held in honor of Bernice's first birthday. They didn't know what day she was born, only that it was during the summer. Seamus had baked little cupcakes and frosted them with pink frosting. He brought the treats into the hangar, where they sat around, eating them. Unimpressed, Bernice remained curled up in her bed by the woodstove, sound asleep.

"I can't believe I am here having a birthday party for a cat," Mr. Finkel grumbled.

"Seamus, what do you want for your birthday this fall?" Fran asked as she picked up a small cupcake from the tray.

"A car," he said.

"You're not getting a car," his father replied.

"Why not? I can use it to deliver the papers."

"No. The government doesn't want us wasting fuel. You have a bike."

"But Papa," Seamus pleaded.

"No arguments. That's final."

"You can take the Scout after I'm gone," Fran said, looking for her father's reaction.

He glared at her.

Seamus sighed and picked up Bernice. He tried to avoid the strained situation between his sister and father as he swirled around the hangar, waltzing with his cat.

"Will you stop fooling with that cat!" Mr. Finkel snapped.

Fran left to walk home. She didn't want to fight with her father and decided it was best to stop speaking to him altogether. Skeeter followed her out and ran to catch up to her.

"Hey," he said.

"Hey, Skeeter. Sorry about that. We're fighting a lot because Papa doesn't want me to fly for the military, and I think that's stupid of him. And selfish."

"He just wants to keep you safe, is all," Skeeter said.

When they were at the Finkel's mailbox, he stopped and looked down at his shoes.

"Fran, I was wondering. Would it be okay to write to you after I'm gone? You don't have to write back. I know you're busy and stuff. It would be nice to have someone to write to."

"Sure," she said, smiling.

He blushed and spun around to walk back to the hangar.

When Fran opened their mailbox and saw the latest issue of her mother's *Women's Home Companion* inside, she couldn't believe it. Right there on the front cover was a photo of a young female pilot wearing a flight suit. She was attractive, with a bright smile, light curly hair and blue eyes.

Her name was Cornelia Fort, and she was working as a flight instructor at Pearl Harbor during the attack. There was an article in the magazine, written by Cornelia, in which she recalled her experience that day. Fran rushed inside of the house and plopped down on the living room sofa. She flipped through the magazine and began reading about Cornelia.

After graduating from one of the most exclusive private schools in the country, she began to take flying lessons. Besides being a recent debutante, she was also a bit of a rebel. In two years, she had earned her private, commercial, and instructor ratings. She had 1,000 hours of flight time as a stunt pilot and as a commercial flight instructor. She was also the first female flight instructor in the state of Tennessee.

Fran wasn't keen on Cornelia being a debutante. Yet she continued reading, intrigued by a female pilot who had as much experience as she.

On the morning of the attack, Miss Fort had a full day of student pilots scheduled for lessons at the John Rodgers Airport in Honolulu. Her first student that morning was hoping to fly solo for the first time.

During the lesson, Cornelia looked for other aircraft on the horizon while her student flew the plane. After completing a few trips around the airport's traffic pattern, she saw a military plane coming in from the ocean. It wasn't unusual since there was a base there, but it surprised her when she realized the plane was heading straight towards them.

Cornelia pushed in the throttle and pulled up on the yoke to get out of its way. She glanced down at the plane now beneath them. That's when she saw the red balls painted on both wings, signifying a Japanese plane.

It was the enemy.

She looked across the horizon and saw hundreds of enemy warplanes coming in straight towards them. One of them dropped something that exploded on impact, blowing up a battleship in the bay area.

As Cornelia tried to lower the plane into the traffic pattern for an emergency landing, she noticed another plane with red circles painted on the wings. She saw sailors rushing around on the battleships as bombs and bullets scattered them in every direction.

Miss Fort landed as machine-gun bullets were riddling their plane. She and her student ran for the hangar and miraculously survived the attack.

A brief appearance of afternoon sun beamed in through the curtains in the living room window, making Fran yawn.

I wish I could have someone like her as a friend.

Fran stretched out on the sofa and closed her eyes. She was sleeping until she felt someone shaking her shoulder.

"Fran, wake up," Seamus said.

She opened her eyes and saw her magazine on the floor.

After dinner, Fran retreated to her bedroom to reread Cornelia's article. She tore out the front page with her photo, tacked it up on her wall, and then went outside to look at the night sky.

It was a clear, moonless night, and the late August sky was filled with stars.

"There are more female pilots out there somewhere," Fran whispered. She smiled at the thought. "And I'm going to find them."

CHAPTER 12

Fran and her father stayed on distant terms over the next few weeks. She knew he was not happy about her stated refusal to sign a government contract to instruct if she should receive one. However, he let her be, and she continued training the student pilots throughout the rest of the summer.

It was a beautiful Saturday in early September and Fran decided to bring Seamus out for a flight to Crater Lake before the colder weather would bring snow to that area. The siblings planned to take Easter and let him fly home once they landed so their father would know they were safe.

The morning air was steadily warming up from the sun's heat, causing steam to rise from the earth. Fran began going over the preflight checklist for the Stearman they had acquired for training purposes.

"What are they?" Seamus asked, pointing overhead to five airplanes flying towards the airport.

Fran looked up, too. They watched as each of the planes landed on the runway, one after another. They were blue and yellow with a clear hatch covering the cockpit, a bold army star painted onto each wing.

"Those are military planes..." she said, her voice trailing off.

A pilot jumped out of one of the aircraft, wearing a tan army flight suit and a parachute strapped to his back.

It was Fran's former boyfriend, John.

He walked up to her and gave her an awkward hug.

She hadn't seen him or heard from him since the breakup. He looked better than she remembered. He used to be pudgy; now, he was lean and muscular.

He must have had to exert some effort in boot camp. They probably made him do stuff like pushups. Or maybe EJ made him go on a diet. I hope she enjoys listening to him talk about his favorite subject: Himself.

Fran chuckled to herself.

"Hell's bells, girl, check this out!" he said, pointing proudly at his plane. "This here is a brand new Vultee Valiant."

He seemed cockier than the John she knew. Fran wasn't sure it was a good thing.

"Nice ride," he continued as he rudely waved his arm straight out at her, "got great visibility in the cockpit and even some protection from the weather. It's way better than trainers like that crummy Cub you fly. Enlisted guys train in these until they step up into pursuit planes and bomber planes."

Seamus came closer.

"Hey, shrimp," John said to him.

Seamus nodded a cool hello.

Fran stroked her hand along the plane's wing. "It's...fabulous," she said.

"Probably the most important trainer the Army Air Force has got," he bragged. "They say just about every military pilot gets trained in a Valiant. Good gosh, that factory is working like crazy! You should see the line of planes they have just waiting for me to deliver."

Fran had noticed the number of army planes flying over the airport had increased. Factories in the country were bustling. In 1939, they had produced six thousand aircraft. However, after the bombing of Pearl Harbor President Roosevelt wanted 100,000 airplanes to be built annually.

John waved impatiently to another pilot, gesturing to fuel his plane next.

"Why aren't you overseas?" Fran asked.

"I'm a ferry pilot for now. I'm delivering planes from factories to military bases. I'll be going over once there's a fighter plane for me to train in. Then I'll fly that plane overseas."

"Where are the factories?"

"Most are on the east and west coasts," he answered. He walked over to his plane as Fran and Seamus followed.

"This plane came from a factory down near LA — me and the boys are taking these up to Seattle. Airplane factories are running twenty-four hours a day, seven days a week."

Once the five aircraft were refueled, John climbed up into his plane's cockpit.

"Say, Fran, you know any pilots that would want to ferry army planes?" he asked. "My commander, Colonel Pitts, he's in desperate need. He'll take any pilot with over five hundred hours."

"Fran has at least five times that," Seamus said.

John rolled his eyes.

"Yeah, but she's a girl, dope. She doesn't count. Gotta fly. Army's waiting on me to deliver this plane to help win the war."

Fran and Seamus backed away from the plane.

"Clear!" John yelled out.

He started the engine, and they both watched as the five pilots taxied down the runway and took off. They could see them out on the horizon, flying side by side in formation.

"You're a way better pilot than he is," Seamus said. "Schmuck."

Fran nodded as they watched the planes fade into the distance.

After seeing John, Fran didn't feel like going all the way to Crater Lake anymore, so she flew them to Corvallis instead. When they landed for fuel, she let Easter free. The bird returned home to their father with a note that read: *We are both safe at Corvallis Airport, coming back home after fueling. — F.*

Fran was quiet at dinner that evening. It was only the three of them.

"Frances," her father said, "thank you for the message from Easter. It was very thoughtful and considerate. I want you to know I appreciated it."

"Sure, Papa."

He looked at her and smiled.

He's trying.

"Anything exciting happen today?" he asked.

"Nope." Fran looked over at Seamus, who wisely chose to ignore his father's question.

"Well," their father said, "while you were away, a delivery boy brought a telegram here for you. It's from the War Department."

He took an envelope from his shirt pocket and placed it on the table. "Frances Finkel" was typed across the front of it.

"Probably offering you a contract to instruct the students. I didn't open it."

She picked up the envelope and looked at it. There was a long silence at the table before she broke it by taking a deep breath.

"Actually," she said. "I just remembered. Something did happen today."

Seamus stopped chewing and held his breath.

"John was at the airport today."

She stood and put her napkin down, picking up her telegram.

"He was flying an army warplane. John was. The same John that flunked his written exam because he was too lazy to apply himself to study. He failed his flight test because he wasn't ready for it. That John is ferrying planes for the army. According to him, there is a desperate need for pilots to deliver these planes. There's a backlog at the factories."

Her father sighed. "Frances, you can do your part by being an instructor for these boys."

"Do you really believe the only task worth me doing is teaching students that can hardly fly to go and get themselves killed?"

"I know you're jealous and bitter about it, but it's not going to make a difference if you — "

"I can't. I won't. It's beyond my comprehension how my being a female constitutes wasting the talent I have to give when it is obvious how much the war effort needs me."

Fran stormed off to her room and threw the unopened telegram on the floor. She shook her head and picked it back up.

"I will not allow these words to convince me to do something I don't believe in," she said. Fran tore up the yellow envelope and what was written inside without reading it. Then she dropped the pieces into her trash bin, turned off her light and fell sleep.

CHAPTER 13

On September 28, Fran turned 18. That morning, she rode the motorbike down to the coast and stopped along the way to buy two white roses. She spent the day walking by the shore, and at sunset, she placed the roses into the water and watched the tide take them out to sea. She rode home as evening fell and then went straight to her bedroom without saying a word to her father or Seamus.

The days grew shorter. Then the rains came.

Autumn turned into winter, giving less opportunity to fly. Army planes continued to land at Seal Rock Airport when they needed fuel or maintenance. Although it was exciting for Fran to see the new aircraft, it also tortured her that the military didn't allow her to fly them.

During the winter months, she sulked around the house and the hangar. Fran listened to the news on the radio and read the newspapers, as she always did. It was mainly about the ongoing war and what citizens could do to help while the boys were overseas fighting. Fran ached to use her abilities to help. At night, she stayed awake until dawn, staring out the window. Fran didn't know why her belief system wasn't getting her anywhere.

She struggled with the negative thoughts that had drifted into her consciousness. She tried to change them by thinking about something positive, but it didn't help; she was still miserable. It was hard for her to be enthusiastic when there didn't seem to be a point to it.

On overcast days when they couldn't take students up for flight lessons, Fran started staying in on the sofa, staring at the clock as her mother used to do. Sometimes she watched the hours go by right into the evening. Eventually, she would sigh and get up to prepare dinner. But that was all. Her father could teach the boys ground school without her, she thought. Fran felt as if someone had snuffed the light out of her soul. She felt trapped and breathless, restless and tired.

One rainy day, in an attempt to shake off her gloomy mood, she forced herself to walk to the hangar. Her father was teaching ground school to the student pilots. Fran sat in the back of the hangar to listen.

"Can someone tell me who discovered instrument flying?" he asked.

"Charles Lindbergh," a student answered.

"Wrong. James Doolittle. Colonel Doolittle was a pilot and a scientist. He was the first pilot to fly blind, meaning he only used the cockpit gauges for navigating. He trained other pilots to do the same. And trust me, once you find yourself flying in the soup, you'll be thankful you learned how to fly using instruments."

Fran knew all about Colonel Doolittle. Her father had met him during flight training when he was in the military and was won over by the man's charisma and chutzpah. He was a legend amongst pilots

— considered by many to be the greatest flier in the world. She wished she could meet him one day. He sounded brave and daring. Unlike her father.

"And boys, once you've enlisted, they'll teach you how to fly in foul weather, but for now, we won't be doing that. You'll be flying overseas soon enough, and then you'll have to do that."

"Just like Charles Lindbergh," a student said.

"Don't use him as a role model," her father snarled. "He's not interested in you going off and fighting to save other people from being persecuted."

"That's right," Fran said, standing up. The students turned to look at her.

"He's an isolationist who only cares about his own family," she said.

Her father glared at her, then folded his arms. He looked over his glasses at Fran and raised one eyebrow.

"How's he any different from you, Papa? You don't want your own to fight in the war, to risk their lives for others. He believes the same. Just keep me home and safe. Let everyone else suffer and die. It's their problem. As long as it's not us they're persecuting, why get involved?"

"Frances, that's enough," he said.

"You're a hypocrite," she said. "You sit here, pretending it's fine that Mr. Gato is working as a farmhand. You think by keeping quiet it will all go away, pass over us. Maybe. Or maybe they'll come for us next."

Disgusted, she marched out of the hangar and walked back to the house.

That night they didn't speak. Fran went to her bedroom after dinner to read. A few minutes later, she heard her father knock on her door.

"Come in," she said.

He stood there, looking at her.

"Frances, you must not be so disrespectful to me, not in front of the students."

"What I said was the truth. I have nothing to be ashamed of. But, maybe you should consider what you are doing. Don't you care about those boys? You're preparing them to die. You know as well as I do that most of them won't make it back home alive. They aren't ready to fly warplanes in a few weeks."

"You don't think I know that?" he hissed. "I think about those boys all the time. Their faces haunt my dreams. Most of the ones we've trained, they're already dead. Maybe one of ten will live or become a prisoner of war or go missing in action."

"I will not sign a contract. I should be out there flying for the army. It's as if I agree that it's fine with me when it isn't."

"Frances, I'm glad you can't join the army. I would never forgive myself if something were to happen to you. I know it's what you want, but it's not what I want. I want to keep my children alive. If you ever fly for the army, you will have no home here."

With that, he softly closed her door.

CHAPTER 14

A few weeks later, Fran was getting ready to head out to the hangar when she heard a knock at the front door.

When she opened it, there stood a tall, slender young woman, wearing a khaki flight suit. She was covered in mud up to her knees.

"I'm so sorry to bother you," she said, "but I was hoping you knew how to get to Seal Rock Airport?"

Fran recognized her immediately and stared, dumbfounded.

"Forgive my manners," the woman said, reaching out her hand. "I'm Cornelia Fort."

Fran shook it numbly.

"My plane is out in that field," she continued, pointing behind her. "I'm afraid it ran out of fuel before I could make it to the airport."

Fran remained silent, still stunned. The young woman's affluence was evident in her mannerisms and speech. Despite her muddy flight suit, Fran found Cornelia to be one of the most gracious and sophisticated women she had ever met.

She definitely comes from money, Fran thought. *Private school education. Lace curtains, that's for sure.*

"Can you help me?" Cornelia asked.

"Yes. I'm pretty sure I can," Fran said, finally able to muster words. "I'll take you to the airport. Wait here."

She went in back to find her boots. Fran knew she'd never get the motorbike, or the truck, out in the field without getting stuck.

"Come on," she said to Cornelia. "We can get enough fuel to fly your plane over to the airport."

They hopped into the Finkel's pickup truck.

"You're the first female pilot I've ever met," Fran told her as they drove to the hangar.

"Ah, there's plenty more of us than me," Cornelia replied.

After they arrived, Fran jumped out of the truck and grabbed a gas container. She filled it at the fuel station, then drove them out to the edge of the field where the plane had landed and parked the truck on the side of the road. As they walked together through the mud, Cornelia recounted her flight.

"Strangest thing," she said. "I was heading north when I noticed the fuel gauge was on empty, so I switched over to the reserve tank. My flight map said Seal Rock was the nearest airport, but I wasn't sure I could make it, so I landed here in this field. I chose a spot away from any roads so there wouldn't be a lot of talk about a female pilot landing a plane in the middle of nowhere. We don't need that in the news right now."

Fran nodded as if she knew what Cornelia was talking about.

"After I landed," Cornelia continued, "I started walking through this very muddy field towards the road. I could see your house, and so

I started heading towards it. I have to say this mud is like quicksand. It kept sucking my boots into it."

"Yep, it's pretty mucky this time of year," Fran replied as they trudged along. "How long have you been a pilot?"

"Oh, gosh, let's see...I had my first flight three years ago when I turned twenty. And I was hooked. I know it sounds silly, but the moment that plane lifted into the air, it was the first time I felt, well, normal. Like I was home. Sometimes when I don't get to fly for a while, I get this nervous feeling like a cat in a room full of rocking chairs," Cornelia said with a chuckle.

"That's how I feel about it, too."

"Are you a pilot?" Cornelia asked.

Fran was about to answer her, but when they came up out of the valley, she saw Cornelia's plane and paused. It was a Vultee, the same type John had flown to Seal Rock Airport. Fran couldn't place her finger on the feeling it gave her, but there was something sinister about it.

A déjà vu — some moment from the past...or the future.

"It's a Vultee," Fran said. "I didn't think women could fly army planes."

"The military just started a secret experimental project that's using women to ferry warplanes," Cornelia explained. "I received a telegram from the War Department, inviting me to join them. They sent one to every female pilot in the country who had over five hundred hours of flight time."

"Is the women's pilot project based in Seattle?" Fran asked.

"I wish. It's at the New Castle Army Base in Wilmington, Delaware. It's much colder out there, especially in the planes with open cockpits."

New Castle Army Base, Wilmington, Delaware, New Castle Army Base, Wilmington, Delaware, Fran repeated the location in her head to memorize it.

They walked over to the plane. Fran placed the fuel container on the ground to have a closer look.

"Most of the airplane factory workers are women," Cornelia said. "They built this entire plane, from the engine block to the rivets."

Cornelia started pouring fuel into the wing, but the tank became full almost immediately.

"Strange," Cornelia said.

"Maybe there's a leak in the wing."

Fran felt around both wings but didn't find any signs of fuel.

"Well then," Cornelia said, "I may as well start it and try to get to Seattle."

She hopped into the cockpit. Fran placed the fuel can behind the seat.

"Just in case," she said.

"You are too kind, my dear. Thank you so very much. It's been lovely meeting you."

The attractive aviator flipped the ignition switch and the propellor blades began to turn as the sound of the engine grew louder. She gave a thumbs-up to Fran, who waved back at her.

The plane rolled down the field, and soon Cornelia soared up and away, into the sky. Fran trudged home through the mud as quickly as she could. She wanted to find the shreds of her telegram, her invitation to fly for the army and tape it back together.

After making it home, Fran took off her muddy boots and rushed to her bedroom. Her trash was empty. *Seamus must have emptied it.*

When he came home from school, her brother told her he'd thrown all the paper into the fireplace that morning.

Her telegram was gone.

CHAPTER 15

Fran slept fitfully that night. She dreamed about a vast flock of birds flying over Crater Lake. The birds darkened the sky. She was swimming in the lake. She swam deeper, down towards the murky bottom. She held her breath as a voice asked, "Are you an evil soul or a good soul?" She woke, gasping for air.

Fran remembered meeting Cornelia and wondered if that, too, was a dream. She thought she felt her hand clutching her telegram, but when she opened it, nothing was there.

Uncle Conrad's book said when thoughts manifested, the results were often even better than what you originally wanted.

She'd met a female pilot. According to Cornelia, there were more. And they were flying planes for the army.

Fran knew what she needed to do.

That morning she was quiet at breakfast. Oregon's overcast and drizzly weather sometimes contributed to her feeling depressed. Only today, it didn't matter to her what the weather was doing.

"I doubt anyone's getting to fly today," she said to her father, trying to sound nonchalant. "I think I'll go into town. May I take the truck?"

"Of course," he said, surprised she was speaking to him again. "Why don't you pick Seamus up after school? Then he doesn't have to walk home in this rain."

After breakfast, Fran drove straight to the First National Bank on Southwest Fifth Avenue in Portland and waited for it to open. Each week while she had worked for her father, he deposited the money she earned. He paid her two dollars an hour and kept track of her hours in the accounting book, where he calculated payroll taxes. When the bank opened, Fran was their first customer. She withdrew five hundred dollars from her savings account and then drove a mile north, following the Willamette River to Portland's Union Station. A large clock sat atop a tower that was part of the station. Like the bank, the station was quite grand inside, with fancy marble floors and polished stone walls. In contrast, though, it was bustling with travelers. Inside, Fran wandered around until she found a line of people waiting to buy tickets.

"May I help you?" the man working behind the window asked her when it was her turn.

"I'd like to buy a train ticket."

"Where to?"

"Wilmington, Delaware."

"The Union Pacific only goes as far as Chicago."

"Then I'll take a ticket to Chicago, please."

"You'll want to ride the streamliner in that case. It's got three sleeping cars with full dining services. You'll get there in two days and one night. Train leaves tomorrow morning and starts boarding at nine o'clock sharp."

"Perfect."

"Round trip?"

"No," she said, shaking her head. "One way."

"A one-way ticket to Chicago on the City of Portland streamliner. That'll be nineteen dollars."

She took a crisp twenty-dollar bill from her wallet and handed it to him. He gave her back a one-dollar bill and a ticket to Chicago.

"Thank you, sir," Fran said as she turned to leave.

"Wait a minute, miss. You know what — you're in luck. There's a new train out in Chicago that goes to the East Coast. It'll take you to Wilmington. Once you get to Chicago's Union Station, look for the Baltimore and Ohio Railroad Station and ask for a ticket to board the Columbian. Got it?"

She nodded. "The Columbian to Wilmington, Delaware. I'll find it."

"You ever been there? Union Station?"

Fran shook her head. She'd never left Oregon.

"Well, let me warn you, it's going to be crazy busy there. Will someone be waiting for you when you arrive in Wilmington?"

She shook her head again.

"Well, that'll be fine, don't worry one bit. You can take a taxi. Give the address to the train attendant, and he'll help you out with that."

Fran smiled at him. "Thank you. You've been very helpful."

"Good luck, young lady. And be careful out there."

After she left the train station, Fran went shopping at the Meier & Frank Department Store and bought a wool-lined leather flight jacket, slacks and a pair of oxford shoes. She looked at dresses on the dress rack but didn't care for any of them.

She ordered a bowl of soup at the uppity Georgian Room restaurant inside of the store. It used to be her mother's favorite place to eat — in Oregon, anyway. She recalled the first time she went there with her mother and her Aunt Elsa. Her aunt ordered an Old Fashioned and then complained about the slow service.

"Honestly, Elsa. How can one live out here?" her mother had asked.

"Why, I believe Oregon would be a spectacular place to live," Aunt Elsa said as they finally brought her drink to the table. "The pine trees, the mountains, the ocean — you know we don't have any of that in New Orleans. And there's no humidity and no bugs. Hallelujah. It's paradise out here, I tell you."

She took a sip of her drink and smiled at Fran.

"My dear niece, you are welcome out to New Orleans any time, but you already know that. You can take over the restaurant for me. I started managing it when I was just eighteen. You can do whatever you want, be anything you want to be. Don't let anyone tell you otherwise, you hear?"

Fran smiled at her aunt as she took a bite of her grilled cheese and tomato sandwich.

"Frances needs to find a husband and settle down," her mother said. "Then she can stop wasting her time with all that airplane nonsense."

"She can still fly an airplane and have a husband. She's just a tomboy, is all. She'll grow out of it."

"How's she going to find a husband while she's up in the sky flying to God only knows where?"

After Fran finished her soup, she continued shopping. She purchased a travel bag and a birdcage for Easter.

She placed her purchases in the back of the truck and drove over to get Seamus at school. He was already walking towards home when she saw him. He looked up with a grin when she honked the truck's horn to get his attention.

"Hey, nice surprise!" he shouted, jumping into the pickup. As they drove home, hard raindrops pelted the truck's windshield. Seamus chattered away about a fight in the cafeteria during lunch, but Fran wasn't listening. She didn't want to tell him she was leaving. She didn't know how to, either.

When they arrived home, Seamus jumped out of the truck, and Fran followed, both of them covering their heads, trying not to get drenched as they headed for the house.

CHAPTER 16

The following morning, Fran waited in her bedroom until Seamus left to pick up his newspapers.

Wearing her new clothes, she crept out into the kitchen as not to wake her father. She was carrying her new overnight bag and Easter in his new travel cage. She put the birdcage down on the table and placed an envelope between the salt and pepper shakers. Then she picked up the cage, took one last look around the house, and stepped outside.

It was still dark as she walked out to the hangar. When she went inside, Bernice was asleep in her bed. The cat had become independent and preferred to stay in the hangar at night. Still, Seamus would occasionally bring her into the house, much to the chagrin of their father.

Fran stroked the purring feline for a moment and then placed an envelope for Seamus on the bed. She knew he'd go there first, after coming back from delivering his papers.

She left the hangar and walked along the road to Newport. Dawn was approaching. The stars began to disappear as night turned into day.

Once in town, she slipped into a diner near the port where the barge that delivered the newspapers docked.

Typically, a handful of people used the barge to hitch a ride into Portland. When people began boarding, Fran left the diner to join them. As the barge backed out of the harbor, she watched the dock receding. Sea lions followed them out of the bay. A few climbed up on rocks, making their dog-like barking sounds as they talked to one another.

The barge drifted under the Yaquina Bay Bridge that connected Route 101. The bridge opened just a few years ago; Fran remembered when she flew over it for the first time. She was with Danny that day. The memory made her feel alone. It was odd for her to go under the bridge; it felt like her world turned upside down.

When the barge docked in Portland, she could see the train station's clock tower not too far in the distance. It was already after nine, and the station was a few blocks uphill. Fran rushed to make it to the train on time. After she gave her ticket to the train conductor, she found her seat and travel compartment and settled in for the two-day trip to Chicago.

She knew her father would be awake by now. He liked to keep on a schedule and woke at the same time every day. He would shower, shave, and comb his hair, then put on an old pair of jeans and a buttoned-down white shirt. When he went into the kitchen, he would find it odd that she wasn't there. He'd start a pot of coffee on the stove. That's when he'd see the note she had left him on the table. Her father would open the envelope and read what she had written:

"It wasn't your fault."

Fran knew he blamed himself for letting them go out flying that fateful day.

She winced at the thought of him reading it, of him realizing she'd left him too, just like her mother had. Maybe never coming back. Perhaps she'd never see him again.

Her mind moved on to Seamus. After delivering his newspapers, he would ride his bike back home. Before going to the house for breakfast, he would stop at the hangar to check on Bernice. That's when he'd find the envelope she had left for him on the cat's bed. In it, he'd see a page torn out from the thought book that read:

"Believe in yourself; believe in everybody; believe in all that has existence."

At the bottom of the page, Fran wrote:

"I'm sorry I can't tell you where I am going, but I think you know.

I promise to write when I can.

All the love there is,

Frances

PART II

"What you seek is seeking you."

— Rumi

CHAPTER 17

Besides Fran, most of the passengers riding the train to Chicago were young sailors or soldiers on their way to military training bases all over the country. She used the time to write a long letter to Seamus, whom she already missed.

Although Fran was on her way to making her dream a reality, she felt selfish for leaving. Each time the train stopped, she considered getting off and going back home. Not because she was afraid, not because she didn't want to go; Fran knew she had no choice. Only she felt torn abandoning her father and brother as her mother had done. The guilt was overpowering. None of them had forgiven Mother, and she doubted there would be any mercy for her.

The sun was rising on the Windy City that wintry day in December, nearly one year after the bombing of Pearl Harbor.

Two days after leaving Oregon, the city of Portland streamliner wound its way through Chicago's western neighborhoods, passing crowds of commuters huddled together for warmth as they waited for their trains.

Gosh, there must be a million people here, Fran thought as the train rolled through the city towards Union Station. She wondered where they were all going — perhaps to work at an office downtown, or to shop, or to attend a college class.

Compared to the beach towns and fishing villages of Oregon's coastline, Chicago's crowds were staggering. It made Fran consider the randomness of life. How meeting another soul among so many — even the briefest encounter, could change one's destiny.

When Fran disembarked, she found the station teeming with a mix of men in uniform and civilians. The train stop was a significant hub for the railways, seeing three hundred trains and over 100,000 passengers through each day.

It was challenging to move in the mob of people with a birdcage and her hand luggage, yet Fran managed to maneuver through the crowd until she found the Baltimore and Ohio station. There, she bought a ticket for the Columbian train to Wilmington.

After boarding the train heading east, she looked out the window as it snaked its way along the southern side of Lake Erie. She forced her mind to picture her benevolent twin. Whenever she did, it surprised her she didn't burst into tears or feel sad at her loss. *Perhaps something's wrong with me. I'm like Mother. Maybe that's how she could leave us.* She recalled how when her mother hugged her, no warmth exuded. *Not like when Aunt Elsa did it. She was a good hugger. She made you feel like she meant it when she hugged you.* Fran wondered how she felt to the person she hugged.

It was late afternoon when the train arrived in Wilmington the next day. When Fran stepped out of the station, she felt the bitter cold blow right through to her bones. She put on her shearling flight jacket and found a row of taxis parked outside the train station. Her first taxi ride ever brought her to the U.S. Army Air Force Base in Wilmington, Delaware. A hand-painted sign at the front entrance read: "Air Transport Control Headquarters," with an arrow pointing to a few buildings at the end of a dirt road.

The taxi driver pulled up next to the guard shack, where a young officer wearing a khaki uniform was waving him over.

"How may I help you?" the guard asked.

"I'm here for the women's squadron," Fran said from the back of the cab.

"Are they expecting you, miss?"

"I'm not sure. Maybe. I received a telegram from the War Department."

"Got it. Project Peanut, no doubt. What's your name?"

After Fran told him her name, he took out a clipboard and searched through the pages on it.

"Huh, that's funny. Frances Finkel — I don't see your name on the list." He shrugged. "I'll call ahead and let them know you're here. Head over to barracks number twelve. It's that building right over there." He pointed to a two-storied building in the distance.

They drove by a large sign that read: "Welcome to New Castle Army Air Force Base." Fran paid the cab driver and got out of the backseat with Easter's cage and her overnight travel bag.

Barracks Twelve appeared recently built and still smelled of fresh wood. Someone had placed a plank across the ice surrounding the entrance for people to walk across and not slip. After living in Oregon her entire life, Fran had grown accustomed to water and mud, but not freezing weather and ice.

She hesitated before opening the barrack's door, wanting to remember the moment. She was about to enter a building for women pilots that flew planes for the army. It all felt surreal — she wasn't sure if she was dreaming.

As Fran headed down the hallway, she saw a woman who looked to be in her late twenties walking towards her. She was stunning, with green eyes and dark wavy hair, and also impeccably dressed. She smiled at Fran as she held out her hand.

"You must be Frances Finkel," she said in a quiet, assuring tone. "My name is Nancy Love. I oversee the women ferry pilots here. It's a pleasure to meet you."

They shook hands. The woman's calm demeanor and delicate looks belied her firm grip, which took Fran by surprise.

"Why don't you have a seat in my office so we can chat?" Nancy suggested as she glided down the hallway. They both walked into her workplace, and she closed the door behind them.

"You brought a bird?" she asked, pointing to Easter's cage.

"Yes, a pigeon," Fran answered. "I taught him to deliver messages for me when I fly."

"Ah. There's a division of the Army Air Corps that trains pigeons to deliver messages, a rather extraordinary group I have heard. So, you are here because you are a pilot looking to fly with us, I assume?"

Fran nodded.

"You must already know — since you're here — we are looking for qualified female pilots to ferry warplanes. However, we don't seem to have you on our list of candidates. I'm not sure why that is. Do you have at least five hundred hours of flight time?"

"I have almost three thousand," she answered.

For a moment, Nancy lost her composure, then quickly regained it.

"Tell you what," she said, "it's late, and you must be tired from your trip, so why don't you stay here overnight with the other women pilots and get some rest? We can conduct your interview first thing tomorrow morning. You'll also need to meet with Colonel Pitts. He oversees the ferrying of aircraft for the army."

"That would be swell," Fran said. "Thank you. I could use a good night's sleep in an actual bed."

"If all goes as planned, we can also give you a flight test, weather permitting. I have another pilot scheduled for tomorrow. She arrived earlier today."

Nancy brought her down the hall, and as they passed a break room, she told Fran she could help herself to coffee and snacks. Fran observed an attractive woman standing in the room, wearing high-heeled pumps and a perfectly tailored suit.

That's one of them. That's one of the pilots.

Fran began to wonder if she would fit in.

Her room had a window, one cot, a metal chair and a wooden two-by-four with hangers for her clothes. She placed Easter's cage on the chair and opened the door. She took out two small metal bowls, filled one with grain and one with fresh water from the bathroom, and then placed them down on the floor. When she flopped down on the bed, she fell asleep, fully dressed.

CHAPTER 18

Fran woke to sunshine peeking in through cracks in the wall of her room. She shivered as she climbed out of bed. She could see her breath.

Fran dressed and went down the hall to the break room, where she found donuts and a fresh pot of coffee. She poured herself a cup of coffee for the first time in her life and nibbled on a chocolate donut. She was nervous about her interview and curious as to why she hadn't seen more women pilots in the barracks.

When she returned to her room, it had warmed up. Easter was on the windowsill, basking in the sun. She smiled and stroked his feathers.

"You can stay here for today and take it easy," she said, leaving the room. On her way to Nancy's office, Fran noticed a mailroom. She returned to get her letter for Seamus and dropped it in the outgoing mail.

When she arrived for her interview, Nancy was in her office, waiting for her.

"Colonel Pitts," she said, "whom you will meet with soon, has a desperate need for pilots to ferry warplanes for the army. But first, let me give you a bit of background on our mission."

She explained how she and Colonel Pitts started Project Peanut, an experimental venture that was using women pilots to fly new planes from factories to military bases.

"Although women may not fly in combat, there isn't any rule against them ferrying warplanes. So I suggested forming a group of the best pilots we could find to prove that women could also fly for the army."

She told Fran that the colonel liked her idea. He asked her to find and vet any available female pilots who could meet their predetermined qualifications and pass a flight test.

They had scoured the Civil Aeronautics Administration pilot's list and found three thousand female pilots. They made a list of those that met their requirements and ranked them in order of hours and ratings.

"Some had already signed government contracts to train recruits to fly, so we had to remove them from our list."

Fran hadn't signed a contract. She breathed a sigh of relief.

"We came up with a final list of one hundred women, and we sent each potential candidate a telegram," Nancy told her. "Cornelia Fort ranked second on the list. Betty Gillies, who is also a dear friend of mine, ranked first. I'm not sure how we missed you, but I'm thrilled to have you here now."

"I have about twenty-five hundred hours myself," Nancy continued, "but I am not ferrying planes right now because I'm overseeing the selection of pilots for Project Peanut."

Fran had wondered if there were any other women pilots like her — she had hoped there were. But what Nancy was telling her now was more than she had ever dreamed possible.

"Did you bring your logbook?" Nancy asked her.

Fran reached into her travel bag and placed a logbook on the desk between them. Nancy picked it up and began thumbing through it. Fran had neatly recorded her hours and aircraft type for every one of her flights as pilot in command.

"Most of the entries I've seen look more like chicken scratches than words," Nancy said. "You're writing is meticulous. I like that. You're careful. But why? What happened that makes you so careful?" she asked thoughtfully.

Fran didn't answer her. Instead, she took out a second logbook from her travel bag and placed it on her desk. Nancy smiled at that. Fran smiled a half-smile back.

After looking through both logbooks, Nancy leaned back in her chair.

"So, you've earned a commercial rating — that's a requirement to fly for us, and a multi-engine rating, which is another rating we are requiring. You also have a transport rating and an instrument rating. Is that all correct?"

"Yes, and I'm also a certified aircraft mechanic."

Fran told Nancy about working in her father's maintenance shop and the many types of aircraft she and her twin brother had maintained.

She also talked about her trips to the coast, describing its beauty, and how much she loved to fly there. When they discussed mechanical issues, Fran lit up on the subject as she recalled some of the problems she'd seen at the hangar. Nancy paid close attention to everything Fran said and appeared pleased she had such an extensive mechanical background. After their conversation ended, Nancy brought Fran over to the room next to hers to meet with the colonel.

As they entered his office, the phone began ringing. A ruggedly handsome officer sitting behind a desk answered it while gesturing for them to have a seat.

"Colonel Pitts, how can I — " he said into the receiver, but before he could finish, the caller interrupted him.

"Do you know how many planes I have waiting here at the factory?" someone on the phone yelled. "When the heck are your pilots coming out to get them?"

"I'm aware of the situation," Colonel Pitts replied. "We're doing the best we can. Unfortunately, every airplane factory in the country is having the same problem."

"Yeah? Well, I don't give a frog's fat ass about that!" the voice said. "I got no place left to put these planes, and I can't keep them inside — we got too many orders to meet! I'm leaving them lined up on the side of the road, for Pete's sake."

"Yep. Yep. Okay," the colonel said. "I'll get someone out there as soon as I can." After the call ended, he glanced over at Fran.

"Look here," he said. He pointed at a chalkboard behind his desk. It had a list of names with ferrying assignments beside them. At least half of the names were crossed out. He stood and crossed out another name.

"Most of these are casualties of crashes," he said, "I'm down to a skeleton crew."

Colonel Pitts told Fran he had flown over 5,000 hours in bomber planes as well as transport planes before being placed in charge of the Air Transport operation. He oversaw the delivery of every aircraft built in factories across the country. He was also responsible for training the pilots to ferry the planes to military bases.

"Most of the pilots have enlisted," he continued. "That leaves me with hardly anyone left to ferry aircraft. And I need experienced pilots to fly these planes, not rookies with less than a hundred hours under their belts."

Nancy stood up to leave. "Colonel Pitts," she said, "this is Frances Finkel."

"I will leave you two alone now," she added, walking out of his office.

"Thanks for showing up, Ace," the colonel said to Fran.

"Ace?"

"I didn't think you were real. Nancy told me you have more flight hours than any of my pilots here."

Fran listened to the colonel as she tried to figure him out. *He has warm eyes, but he's no cream puff.*

"Most of my ferrying pilots went overseas after Pearl Harbor. In the meantime, the number of aircraft being built is astronomical. I just can't keep up."

Colonel Pitts ran his hand across his cropped haircut.

"Long story short, I need more pilots. All I can get. As long as you have the credentials and you're a good pilot, that's all I care about. Women are just as good pilots as men in my book. Maybe better." He stood up, walked to the front of his desk, then leaned in close to Fran.

"I need pilots that won't risk these ships," he continued. "I need these planes delivered intact, understand? That's your job. That's it. You don't need to be some hero. And I especially don't want a show-off or a daredevil."

Fran nodded that she understood.

"You ready for your flight test?" he asked, and she nodded again.

Colonel Pitts carried a clipboard with him as they went outside together. They were heading towards the runway when a young man with a severe case of acne approached the colonel and saluted him. He looked barely 18.

"I'm getting shipped overseas," he told the colonel. "Leaving tomorrow. I'm sorry, I know how short-handed you are, sir."

The colonel sighed and shook his head.

"Was he a pilot?" Fran asked after the cadet left.

"Even worse, he was one of my airplane mechanics. I've never had enough airplane mechanics to begin with, and now I've just lost another one."

They walked over to the flight test certifier, a heavyset officer with a bored look on his face. He was preparing to take Catherine, a short woman with kinky hair, for her flight test. The colonel told Fran that she had been teaching aerobatics before receiving her telegram.

They stood by and watched as Catherine went over a preflight checklist for the airplane.

Fran smiled when she saw the plane. She was in luck. It was a Piper Cub.

"I'm going to need you to train alongside my male pilots," Colonel Pitts said to Fran. "You'll fly much bigger planes than that trainer there — fighter planes, attack bombers and fast planes — pursuit planes that only have one seat. That means you'll be alone for your first flight lesson. Think you can do all that, Ace?"

"Yes, sir," Fran said. "I do."

Catherine hopped into the plane's back seat as the flight test certifier squeezed into the front seat.

"Say, you sure you know how to fly a plane?" he kidded.

Catherine didn't answer him. Instead, she flipped the ignition switch, pressed her feet down firmly on the rudder pedals, and turned the key to start the plane. The engine rumbled as the propeller began to spin. Colonel Pitts and Fran watched her taxi towards the runway, snapping her chewing gum.

A few minutes later, Catherine was flying over them. She flew straight up and then dove towards the runway before she pulled up again. She performed a series of dramatic spins and loops as Fran and Colonel Pitts watched their private air show. Fran couldn't believe it. It was the first time she'd seen anyone perform aerobatics in a Cub.

She flew up high again and turned the plane upside down. As the plane fell nose-first towards the earth, she pulled up and did three tailspins and then a full loop.

"Is that part of the test?" Fran asked as they continued to watch.

"Uh...I don't know," Colonel Pitts stammered as he searched through his clipboard. "I didn't think so."

Ten minutes later, she landed on the runway and taxied the plane up beside them. The flight test certifier jumped out, holding his stomach.

Catherine, excited from the adrenaline rush, was chewing her gum fast as he ran behind the hangar to get sick.

"Hey!" she yelled after him. "Did I pass or what?"

"You passed," Colonel Pitts told her. "Finkel, I'll give you your flight test. Let's just get this done. I haven't time for horseplay."

He had her take the plane to an altitude of 2,000 feet, stall the engine, recover, and then perform a few gentle turns. After that, he gave her the signal to land, and she brought the plane down onto the runway with a perfect touchdown. The colonel told Fran to let Nancy know she had passed her flight test.

When Fran arrived at her office door, Nancy was on the phone with Colonel Pitts.

"She was showing off," Fran heard the colonel saying. "I can't have it. I know she's a good pilot, but we're going to need to retrain her."

Fran waited for their conversation to end before she walked in. Nancy smiled at her and gestured for her to have a seat.

"How did it go?" Nancy asked.

"I passed," Fran said.

Nancy smiled, then tilted her head to one side.

"You know, you look young for twenty-one," she said.

"That's because I'm not," Fran said. "I'm eighteen."

Nancy's face grew serious. "The minimum age for Project Peanut pilots is twenty-one."

"But the male pilots, their minimum age is eighteen. I don't understand."

"I'm sorry, Frances."

CHAPTER 19

After learning she wasn't old enough for Project Peanut, Fran headed to her room to pack up her belongings and get Easter. On the way, she began to consider what she could possibly do now. *I'll go to New Orleans — I could always work in the kitchen at my aunt and uncle's restaurant.*

When Fran walked into her room, she found a petite girl there, looking at Easter.

"Say," she said, "this sure is a beautiful bird."

"He's a pigeon," Fran said. "He may be a passenger pigeon, but I'm not sure."

"Nice to meet another female pilot," the girl said with a grin. "We need all the help we can get. I'm Betty."

Fran shook her head and looked away.

"What's wrong?" Betty asked.

Fran told her they couldn't accept her as a pilot for Project Peanut because she was too young.

"What? Let me can talk to Nancy. Can you stick around until we can get them to change the rule?"

"Sure. If they would let me stay."

"Nancy and I go way back. Maybe we can find another job for you here."

Suddenly, Fran had an idea. She remembered Colonel Pitts needed mechanics — maybe he'd let her take the place of the one who had left that day. She told Betty, who said it sounded like a great idea. They walked back over to Nancy's office to see if it was possible.

Catherine was there when they walked in. She gave Fran a thumbs up.

"Nice flying out there!" Catherine said. "Looking forward to working with you."

"Catherine," Nancy began.

"Call me CC. Everyone does."

"CC, the future of women flying for the military depends on the success of this project. I know you're used to flying outside of the envelope, but we can't afford to have a risk-taker on our team. You'll have to fly conservatively when you ferry planes for the army."

"I understand, Mrs. Love."

"Please, call me Nancy." She looked up at Betty and Fran standing in her doorway.

"Betty, you know I don't make the rules," Nancy said, "and I know it makes little sense that women pilots need to be twenty-one while the men only need to be eighteen. If I can get her into Project Peanut, I will. I promise."

"Yeah, yeah," Betty said, "but are there any age restrictions for mechanics?"

Nancy stood up. "Let's go find out."

All four of the women went to see Colonel Pitts in his office.

"She's eighteen," Nancy said.

He looked at Fran, then sighed. "That's a shame. I need you."

"Did you know she's also a mechanic?" Nancy said. "Are there any age restrictions for female mechanics?"

"Well, the thing is," Colonel Pitts said, scratching his head, "since we don't have any female airplane mechanics, I would have to say that there aren't."

"I'll do whatever I can to help," Fran said. "I'm an excellent mechanic, and you said so yourself that you needed one."

Nancy and Colonel Pitts looked at each other.

"She can stay in the women's barracks," Nancy said.

"I don't see why not," Colonel Pitts said. "I'll have our lead mechanic get you up to speed."

Fran decided at that moment that no matter what her present circumstances may be, she would refuse to expect anything but the best outcome she could imagine. And that was to one day fly for Project Peanut.

When Fran returned to the barracks, several women were having coffee in the break room. Cornelia Fort was one of them. Fran noticed how she held her mug with such grace and ease. Cornelia recognized her immediately. She set down her coffee and strolled across the room.

"Well, if it isn't my savior from Oregon!" she exclaimed. "Nancy just told me you were here. Why didn't you tell me you were a pilot, silly?"

Fran shrugged and smiled sheepishly.

Gertrude, the attractive woman Fran had seen yesterday afternoon in the break room, told her she was just in time for their first mission. "We're going to the Piper Factory in Pennsylvania in a couple of days to pick up planes and ferry them out to Long Island."

"I'm not flying," Fran said. "Not yet anyway," she quickly added. "I am going to be working here, only just as an airplane mechanic."

"Well, I don't know of any other female airplane mechanics, so it's not 'just' anything," Gertrude said. "I, for one, am very impressed."

Fran blushed, embarrassed by all the attention. *Maybe these debutantes aren't so bad.*

"Let's all meet in Gertrude's room for a libation after dinner," Cornelia said as they were leaving the break room. "She has a full bar!"

"Come on," Betty said and grabbed Fran's arm. "You must be hungry. Let's get something to eat in the officers' club."

It wasn't until she saw the variety of food in the serving line that Fran realized she was starving. She loaded up her tray with mashed potatoes, roasted carrots, fried chicken and apple pie. Betty led the way over to a table where Nancy and CC were already seated. After she sat down and started eating, Fran wasn't sure if it was just because she was so hungry, but she found the food in the officers' club delicious.

"Mikey wrote that he'd be able to get a few days of leave in a month," CC said. Mikey was CC's husband and a fighter pilot as well. "He asked if he can swing by so we can get together."

"Let me see if I can get Colonel Pitts to buy into that first," Nancy replied. "I mean, really — you just got here."

"Frances, are you married or engaged?" Betty asked.

Fran had her mouth full as she shook her head. Cornelia came over and sat next to Fran.

"See that," Cornelia said. "she's smart like me. Nobody's going to clip her wings."

"That's okay, there's plenty of fish in the sea," CC said, nodding at the room full of men. "Just look at this place — can't throw a rock without hitting a good-looking guy."

"I was almost engaged, but it was all happening too quickly," Cornelia said. "I wasn't sure if he was the right one."

"How do you know if someone's the right one?" Fran asked.

CC smiled. "It's a feeling you get. Once you've felt it, you just know."

"It's called Cupid's arrow," Betty said, laughing. "It strikes in an instant."

"But don't marry the first guy that gives you goosebumps," CC said. "Try to find a guy who has the same vision. Someone who sees the road ahead as you do."

"My husband tells everyone I'm a better pilot than he is," Nancy added. "It's rare for a guy to admit something like that. He brags about it, even. Some guys can't handle it if a woman can outdo them, but the good ones are attracted to a woman whose talent shines through."

"Those are keepers all right," Betty said.

After dinner, Fran checked on Easter and then headed down the hall. As she got closer to Gertrude's room, she could hear laughter. When she went inside, she met Doris, who was also going on the Piper mission.

"Frances, what can I get for you?" Cornelia asked as she was pouring drinks.

It was true; Gertrude had a full bar. Fran stared at the bottles but didn't know what to say. She'd never drank alcohol.

"Uh, it's Fran," she stammered.

"Well, Fran," Cornelia said, "you know what I do when I can't decide what I want? I order champagne. Because you know they'll have to open a fresh bottle, and it's champagne — it goes with brunch, lunch, dinner, celebrations — heck, it goes with everything!" She pulled a bottle of champagne out of an ice bucket and began turning its wire cap.

"It always takes six turns of the wire," she continued. "I know. I've watched a lot of these get opened." She popped the cork and poured a glass of champagne for each of the women.

"Ladies," Betty announced. "I'd like to make a toast to our newest addition."

"But I'm not really one of you," Fran said. "I'm not a pilot for the army."

"Doesn't matter," Doris said. "You're still one of us!"

Betty held up her glass.

"A toast! To the army's only female airplane mechanic, Fran Finkel!"

The ladies lifted their glasses to toast Fran, who then had her first taste of champagne.

CHAPTER 20

On Fran's first day of work, the chief aircraft mechanic showed their newest mechanic around the army base hangars as he introduced her to the other mechanics. During her training period, Fran worked hard and asked lots of questions. The mechanics quickly accepted her as one of them and were pleased to have someone sharing the workload.

Since Fran worked as an aircraft maintenance mechanic, she was allowed to reside in the women's barracks. Although she wasn't flying, the ladies still considered her to be one of them.

And that meant the world to Fran.

Over the next few weeks, more female pilots joined them in their barracks. A total of twenty women made up Project Peanut, with Fran being the youngest.

Fran loved being surrounded by other female aviators for the first time in her life. Back in Oregon, she had only known male pilots. Most of the women were from wealthy homes, which was how they could afford airplanes and flight lessons. They'd also graduated from elite schools such as Sarah Lawrence, Bryn Mawr, Wellesley, Radcliffe and

Vassar — the school Fran's mother had attended, which in some way made them feel like family. Still, Fran's lack of exposure to an aristocratic life made her feel like an outsider.

Fran found Nancy to be unlike the other girls, not that anyone would have used the word 'girl' to describe her. And she was as cool as a cucumber. If you had to fly across the ocean, Nancy Love would be the one to choose as your copilot. She was quiet and thoughtful but didn't wear her heart on her sleeve. Instead, she kept to herself and didn't show her emotions.

CC was the funny and outspoken one. She could also be dramatic, flying off the handle about how some guy's bad flying nearly killed her. She was from New Jersey and had the accent as proof. When she had met her husband, she told them it was love at first sight. CC was crazy about him. She took any opportunity to bring Mikey into their conversation so that she could have the chance to talk about him.

They all mothered Fran, except Cornelia, who was closest to her in age. Miss Fort was from a prominent and wealthy home. She had even had her own chauffeur. The young aristocrat reminded Fran of an exotic bird; Cornelia found everyone interesting, including Fran, who adored her. Like Danny, Cornelia kept a journal that she always carried with her. She found Cornelia to be an introspective soul, much like her twin. Their obsession with words, Fran thought. She'd never had a sister but imagined it would be something like how she felt about Cornelia.

Although keeping busy with the planes that needed maintenance, in the back of Fran's mind was the constant concern over Seamus. She worried about how he was doing without her. She had written him three letters but had no way of knowing if he received them.

What if Papa was reading them first?

One day she phoned the house when she thought her brother might be there, only her father answered it. She didn't respond when she heard him say hello. Fran wasn't expecting to hear his voice. He never picked up the phone.

"Frances?" he had said.

She hung up, her heart racing. She couldn't bear to hear what her father would say to her.

CHAPTER 21

After her first month of working as a mechanic at the base, Fran finished the maintenance check of a Twin Beech airplane all by herself. The ship was one of the transport planes used to fly officers to other bases. They dubbed the fleet "Snafu airlines."

Although the mechanics may have accepted Fran as one of them, it didn't mean the male pilots had. None of them would fly in the Twin Beech once they knew a woman had performed the maintenance check.

When Colonel Pitts heard that, he flew the ferry pilots out to the Piper factory in the Twin Beech to prove to the male pilots he had complete confidence in Fran's abilities. And although it was acceptable to fly with Colonel Pitts, Nancy warned the women of traveling unescorted with a male pilot.

"No reason for creating any gossip," she had emphasized. Because Project Peanut was not public knowledge yet, the women pilots were asked to maintain a low profile.

Nancy had also instructed them not to fly in formation like the male ferry pilots often did. She preferred they stay at least 500 feet away from each other. She didn't want any accidents. Taking unnecessary risks for fun wasn't acceptable — not for Project Peanut. Fran knew this because CC told her everything to keep her in the loop.

Over the next month, Fran watched the Project Peanut pilots go through the same training as the men. They attended ground school to learn about flight instruments, cross-country navigation, emergency procedures and flight maneuvers. Fran would sit in on the training after her workday ended. Even though she wasn't flying yet, she still believed she would.

One evening after a long day, Fran took a seat in the back of a training class already in progress. The instructor, Sergeant Arnold, was reviewing army flight hour requirements. Fran read along as he wrote them out on the blackboard.

The meager amount of flight time pilots received before they went overseas appalled her. She stood and went up to the instructor. He was tall, almost a head taller than she.

"Excuse me," Fran said. "but that just isn't right."

The officer raised his eyebrows at her. "Of course it is. There's primary training, then basic training and advanced flight training. After that, it's off you go, overseas."

"After only two hundred hours of flight time?" she asked. "I don't mean you're wrong, I mean that amount of time, well it's just...it's insufficient."

"Listen here, miss. I don't make the rules," he said.

"I hear that a lot," she replied.

He chuckled, amused.

"Yeah, well, so who the hell are you?" he asked.

"I'm one of the mechanics. But I'm also a pilot."

"So, why aren't you out ferrying?"

"I'm only eighteen."

"Well, so what's that got to do with anything? These guys are all eighteen."

"The people who are in charge decided. You know — the ones that make the rules."

"Then you think you should be out there flying for us?"

"Yes, as a matter of fact, I do."

"Really? Huh, we'll just see about that then."

CHAPTER 22

Soon after her run-in with the night school instructor, Colonel Pitts called for Fran to come to his office. Nancy was already there; both of them were waiting for her when she walked in.

"Last week," the colonel said, "you were in a training class with an instructor, Sergeant Arnold. I heard you had an argument with him about flight time?"

Fran nodded. "The tall one?"

"Yes, that one. It seems you made quite an impression on my commanding officer's son. He wanted to know why you aren't out there, ferrying planes."

Colonel Pitts told her Sergeant Arnold was the son of General Arnold, who was in charge of the entire U.S. Air Force.

"The general said we should also look into using any qualified women pilots who are over eighteen that have over five hundred hours of flight time."

He paused. Fran held her breath, waiting.

Then the colonel grinned at her.

"You're in, Ace."

Fran jumped up out of her chair. "You mean I can fly planes for the army?"

"Congratulations and welcome to Project Peanut," Nancy said. Fran couldn't help herself; she threw her arms around Nancy and hugged her.

"You'll need a tailor to fit you for a uniform as soon as possible," Nancy told her, "they ask that you wear it for public appearances. You'll also receive a flight suit and parachute to wear when flying."

Colonel Pitts told Fran she would have to commit to the project for three months. After that, she could leave if she wanted, but he may ask her to continue to fly for them, based on the situation.

"Thank you, sir!" she said to Colonel Pitts. "You won't regret it, I swear! I'll be the best pilot you have, I promise!"

"All I ask is that you please try to keep a low profile. I don't want it looking like you're getting any special attention while you're on my squad."

Fran ran out of the office to tell the others, but they were all delivering planes.

On her first official day on the job as a Project Peanut pilot, Fran went to the tailor downtown to be fitted for her uniform. The outfit comprised a gray-green wool top, wool slacks, a skirt and a foldable cap.

When she looked at herself in the mirror in her uniform, she grinned.

"Gee whiz," she said to her reflection, "and they said this girl wouldn't fly planes for the army, but would you look at that?"

While in town, she also purchased a navy-blue dress and a pair of black patent leather heels. After seeing how the other women dressed, she decided she needed to upgrade her wardrobe.

While her uniform was being tailored, she found a grain store and bought a bag of grain for Easter.

When Fran returned to the barracks, she went to Nancy's office to learn about her first assignment.

The plan was for her to join four other women to ferry five new Cubs from the Piper factory to an army base in Long Island. Nancy showed Fran how to fill out the paperwork for each plane's receipt and delivery.

She also told Fran they based Project Peanut in Delaware because it was close to the factories in the Northeast, the ones that had the largest backlogs of trainer planes that the nearby army bases were waiting for.

"What about the army bases all over the rest of the country?" Fran asked. "Don't they need trainer planes?"

"Colonel Pitts and I are working on that, trust me," Nancy answered and winked at her.

Although the other women pilots had already made the trip to the Piper factory several times, it would be the first time for Fran. When they arrived to pick up the planes, it surprised her to see that most of the workers were women.

It also surprised the factory workers to see female pilots. They couldn't stop staring as the five women dressed in full uniform walked across the factory floor to check out the planes.

When airplane orders hit the roof and men went off to fight in the war, the factories hired women to meet the demand. Once the women workers were up to speed, they assembled the planes ahead of schedule, which caused a logistics issue where hundreds of aircraft sat parked outside of factories, waiting for pilots to bring them to their destination.

After completing the paperwork and going over their checklists, each of the five women pilots started up a Piper Cub and then flew off towards the army base in Long Island.

For Fran, it was her first flight as an army pilot. She should have felt overjoyed, but the bitterly cold air that winter night took away any thrill. Fran tried not to focus on the fact that she was freezing, but all she could think about was frostbite.

When they arrived at the army base, the supervising officer accepting the aircraft was furious.

"I needed these planes two months ago!" he shouted at them. "Where have you been?"

"Just following orders," CC told him with a smile as they walked away. "We have other bases that need planes. We can only be in one place at a time."

Fran spent the next several weeks delivering trainer planes from the Pennsylvania factory to army bases in southern states. Although the travel was exhausting and the weather was freezing, she loved every minute. The ferry pilots would take a train or a bus to the airplane factory, complete the required paperwork, and then go over each step of the checklist to ensure the plane was airworthy. Then, using flight maps, the women would find the aircraft's army base destination, and once again, there would be more paperwork to fill out. To return to their barracks, they took a train or a bus. They would stay overnight in a hotel if they had to because of train schedules. They also did so when foul weather kept them grounded in an area for days.

One night after a grueling trip, CC, Cornelia and Gertrude decided to stay overnight in Virginia at a hotel near the train station. When they entered the hotel, a sign in the lobby read: "No Jews."

Fran's heart raced. She recognized several of the male pilots who were waiting in the check-in line as well. *What if this causes a stir? Colonel Pitts won't like it one bit. He'll send me packing.*

When it was her turn, the hotel attendant waited for her to speak.

"I'd like a room, please," she said, looking away.

"How many people?" he asked.

"Just one," she said.

"I'll need a photo ID, young lady. You need to be eighteen to stay here alone."

She put down her pilot's license. When the front desk attendant saw her name, he scowled.

"You can't stay here," he said. "Didn't you read the sign out front? We don't want you people in our hotel."

CC began pushing her way to the front of the line.

"I just saw a rat running down the hallway out here!" CC hollered.

"We'll get a room someplace else," she said, glaring at the attendant. She grabbed Fran by the arm and headed for the door. "Let's go, fly girl."

"What's wrong?" one of the male pilots asked Fran. "They out of rooms?"

Fran stopped. "No," she said, loud enough so everyone could hear. "I'm Jewish, and they don't allow Jews to stay here."

"Wait a minute!" Cornelia exclaimed. "Then I'm leaving, too!"

"You don't have to do that," Fran said. "Really."

Gertrude shook her finger at the attendant.

"Why do you think we're all out here in the middle of the night?" she said. "We're fighting a war against this sort of thing, in case you didn't know."

Gertrude and the rest of the pilots, including the men, left the line and stood by Fran.

"We're going, too," one of the male pilots said. "If you can't stay here, then we're not staying here, either."

The pilots all left together and walked down the street until they found another hotel. The rooms cost more than the first hotel, but there were two double beds and a sofa in each of them. The guys split the cost of one room, and the girls did the same.

The women settled in for the night, and CC told crazy stories that made them laugh so loud that the people in the room next to theirs pounded on the wall for them to be quiet.

CC and Gertrude took one bed, Fran and Cornelia took the other one, and then everyone tried to sleep.

"Cornelia," Fran said in the dark. "You awake?"

"Yes, what is it?"

"Do you have a sister?"

"No, only brothers. How about you?"

"Just brothers, I mean just a brother." She didn't want to talk about Danny for fear she would break down and get emotional. The thought of Seamus also caused a pang of guilt. She sent positive thoughts out to her little brother, promising that she'd return home one day. Somehow. And on that thought, Fran fell asleep.

CHAPTER 23

Several weeks after Fran started flying planes for Project Peanut, the ferry pilots caught up on the backlog of trainer planes at the East Coast airplane factories. Once they did, Colonel Pitts re-assigned Cornelia back to the California base where she had been located when she and Fran first met.

Fran remained in the Northeast, where the weather continued to grow even colder. The temperature was below zero the day she went out to ferry one of the PT-19s waiting for her at the Fairchild factory in Maryland. Until now, Fran had only ferried planes with other pilots. This would be her first trip alone.

The PT-19 was bigger than a Cub and had a larger fuel tank, which meant fewer stops. Unfortunately, it also had an open cockpit.

When flying, Fran wore fleece-lined leather gloves and a wool scarf, to protect exposed areas of her face from frostbite. She also brought Easter with her whenever she delivered a plane alone. Fran could send him off with her location if she had an emergency and needed to land in a remote area. She kept him in a small canvas bag she wore under her flight suit. Although Easter didn't seem to mind the cold at all, even at 3,000 feet, Fran didn't want him out in the open cockpit.

When she arrived at the factory, she found the plane parked outside, waiting for her. Fran went inside to complete the paperwork and get warm. Then she went back out to complete her checklist, despite the bitter temperature. However, when she tried to start the engine, there was a problem.

Fran could hear the engine groaning, but it didn't seem to have enough power to turn the propeller blades. After a few unsuccessful attempts, she went back into the factory to look for some help. She found a young woman up on a ladder, drilling rivets into the body of an airplane.

"Excuse me," Fran said, "do you know if there's someone who works here that could come outside and help me start an airplane?"

The woman looked down from the ladder.

"Who are you?" she asked.

"I'm the pilot."

Several women on the factory lines who were in earshot stopped what they were doing and looked over.

"Did you say you were the pilot?" the woman asked.

Fran nodded. Another woman on the factory line stopped to watch them and nudged the worker next to her.

"Hey," she said, pointing at Fran. "Look there. The pilot's a girl."

The woman on the ladder gestured to a closed door. "The engineers are in back, hanging out in their workshop."

When Fran opened the shop's door, she found a few men seated at workbenches, smoking cigarettes. The shelves behind them were overflowing with aircraft parts.

"Hey there, doll face," one of them said. "What can we do for you?"

"The plane won't start," she said to him.

"Where's the pilot?"

Here we go again. Fran sighed. "I'm the pilot."

They stared at her without moving until a dark-haired boy with green eyes stood up.

"It sometimes happens this time of year," he said, crushing out his cigarette. "That's the last plane of the lot. The other pilots who were here yesterday left that one. It's been sitting out there a while. Let's get it inside so it can get warm. I think maybe it's been out in the cold for too long, is all."

The engineer led Fran outside to the plane, and they both pushed it into the building.

While she waited for the PT-19 to warm up, Fran wandered through the manufacturing area. The sheer volume of aircraft at various stages of assembly astounded her. As she walked along the factory lines, it grew quiet. Many of the women stopped working to stare at her.

The amount of attention she was receiving for being a female pilot surprised Fran. Then she remembered her own amazement at the sight of Cornelia on her doorstep back in Oregon.

"She looks like something from right out of the movies," a worker whispered as Fran walked by.

When the helpful engineer thought enough time had passed for the engine to have thawed, they opened up the large metal doors and pushed the plane back outside. As the cold air rushed into the factory, Fran hopped into the cockpit and flipped the ignition switch. The engineer grabbed the propeller's blade and swung it down. This time the engine started. The propeller began turning faster and faster as it gained speed.

Suddenly, Fran heard clapping and cheering coming from behind her. When she turned to look, she saw over a hundred women standing outside in the cold, watching her. She blushed, embarrassed by so much attention.

Fran turned and looked straight down at the long, dark road ahead, but before she pushed the throttle forward to taxi into the frigid weather, she leaned out and gave the ladies a thumbs-up sign. The gesture made them cheer even louder. She grinned back at them.

"Come on, Easter," she said, rolling away from the factory. "Let's get this ship delivered."

CHAPTER 24

It took three days for Fran to deliver the PT-19 to its destination at a Tennessee military base. After completing her mission, she hitched a ride back to the East Coast in an army transport plane.

When Fran arrived at her home base in Delaware, Colonel Pitts asked her to come to see him and Nancy in his office.

"I got a call from the guy in charge of accepting planes at the base in Tennessee where you just delivered a Fairchild," he said when she sat down. "He was wondering why it was taking so long for the rest of the planes to arrive." He looked at the schedule on the blackboard. Nineteen pilots, who had left days before her, were also out ferrying ships from the same batch built in the Fairchild factory.

"Seems you managed to deliver the first plane." He scratched his head. "And you left days later than the other pilots."

"Is that bad?" she asked.

"No. It's just unbelievable. I think it's some kind of record."

"I figured out what altitude had the fastest tailwind and flew it."

He looked over at Nancy and nodded.

"We have some news for you," Nancy said.

"I am relocating you," the colonel said, "along with Nancy and CC. You'll be joining Cornelia at the army base in Long Beach, California. It's close to the Lockheed, Northrop and Vultee factories."

Fran's heart raced. She knew those were the factories building bomber and pursuit planes.

Nancy told Fran they planned to redistribute the Project Peanut pilots to different parts of the country to cover areas where other factories needed pilots to ferry planes. After delivering the backlog of primary trainer planes, they could now move forward to help deliver bigger planes designed to travel greater distances. Colonel Pitts had chosen his best pilots for the assignment. Those selected pilots would train to fly planes to military bases all over the country.

Fran couldn't believe what she was hearing; not only would she be able to leave the cold weather behind her, but she would be flying bigger planes. It was her dream come true. She was also happy for CC because it meant she might get to see Mikey at his base in LA. If she did, it would be the first time she had seen her husband since she started ferrying planes for the army.

It didn't surprise Fran that the colonel selected Nancy to ferry the larger aircraft. Nancy was one of the best female pilots in the country. The four of them would receive the same training as the male pilots, and once they passed their check-ride, they would begin ferrying fighter planes. Fran couldn't wait to get out of the cold weather and start training in the bigger, faster aircraft.

Soon after resolving the trainer plane shortage on the East Coast, Colonel Pitts received a promotion to Brigadier General. He also moved to the West Coast to oversee pilot training and coordinate the delivery of the pursuit and bomber planes.

It was late January when the three female pilots joined Cornelia in warm, sunny Long Beach. Fran, Cornelia, Nancy, and CC shared a small two-bedroom house on the base that served as a barracks for them. Each of the bedrooms had two bunks. Cornelia and Fran shared one bedroom, while Nancy and CC shared the other.

After completing several weeks of training, Fran started ferrying Vultee airplanes. The same type of aircraft Cornelia and John had been ferrying when she saw them for the first time.

Each morning as the sun came up through the coastal fog, Fran would climb into an army jeep that brought the ferry pilots out to the Vultee factory. Then, after completing the paperwork and a pre-flight checklist, she would fly the new aircraft to its destination. Soon she was traveling all over the West Coast, sometimes with a small group of pilots, but most of the time, she flew alone.

Many of the pilots needed to be trained to read gauges when flying in poor weather. Fran, however, already had an instrument rating and knew how to fly using only gauges.

What she didn't know was that she was about to become the first female pilot to fly a pursuit plane.

When General Pitts came out to the women's barracks that morning, he found Fran alone, studying. Cornelia was out delivering a Valiant trainer plane to an army base in Washington, CC was attending instrument training school and Nancy was on her way back to the base via Snafu airlines.

"Do you think you can fly the P-39?" the general asked.

"Is that the one the guys call the flying coffin?" Fran replied.

She'd heard about the plane from the other pilots. It terrified most of them.

"It's capable of speeds up to four hundred miles per hour," he said. "The Bell P-39 Airacobra is one of the fastest pursuit planes on the planet. It's an excellent plane — "

"If flown precisely as designed," Fran said, interrupting him. "Otherwise, it can be rather unforgiving of the slightest payload error, which turns it into one of the deadliest planes on the planet."

He rolled his eyes and sighed.

"It's just tricky to master the pitch angle. It's not a bad plane. I believe you can fly it. Do some research and see what you can learn and then find me after that. We can go over the plane together."

He wants me to prove it's a safe plane to fly.

Fran went to the hangar where the pilots were attending training classes. She asked an instructor for the P-39 pilot manuals and brought them back to her room. She studied the plane's manuals all morning until she had them memorized. Then Fran located a P-39 in one of the hangars and spent a few hours inside the cockpit, studying the controls.

It would be the largest and fastest ship she had ever flown. Fran couldn't wait to get up in the sky.

Later that afternoon, General Pitts came out to review the P-39 with Fran.

"What's the wingspan?" he asked.

"Thirty-four feet," she answered.

"Max speed?"

"Uh, three hundred and seventy-six miles per hour."

"V-N-E?"

"Four hundred and seventy-five."

She pulled a piece of paper out from her pocket.

"What's that?" he asked.

"I wrote my own checklist," Fran replied. "I used the information from the tech manuals. Is that okay?"

He nodded, then climbed up on the wing and opened the plane's door.

"Get in," he said. Fran climbed up the wing and got inside. Once she had settled into the cockpit, the general placed a blindfold over her eyes.

"Where's the fuel indicator switch for the tanks?" he asked.

She put her hand on it.

"The throttle?"

She found it.

"The altimeter?"

She put her hand over it.

The general went through every switch and gauge, asking her to find it. Without hesitating, Fran did.

"What do you think?" he asked her.

"I can fly it," she answered.

"Why don't you get suited up then."

On her way over to get her flight suit and parachute, Fran ran into John Sorenson.

"I hear you're training in pursuit planes now," he sneered. "We had fifty fatalities last month — half of those were in a P-39. Good luck! You're gonna need it."

Fran knew John was still ferrying the trainer planes because he hadn't completed the instrument training necessary to move up to the bigger planes, but she didn't say a word. Instead, she ignored him and continued to head to her room.

When she returned to the hangar, General Pitts had already gotten the mechanics to bring the P-39 outside. The sun was setting, and the desert air was crisp and clear.

While going through her checklist, Fran noticed the fuel was close to empty. She decided to make this a short flight as she climbed into the cockpit. The general began to walk away, then stopped.

"By the way," he said over his shoulder, "you'll be the first female pilot to fly one of these, in case you didn't know."

Fran looked around the area.

"Clear!" she called out, warning any bystanders that she was about to start the engine.

She flipped the ignition switch and pressed down on the starter pedal. The propeller blades began turning as the engine rumbled.

She smiled and drew in her breath.

First female pilot. Do not screw this up.

She adjusted her goggles and gave the thumbs-up signal to the general. After letting the engine warm up, she taxied over to the runways as she talked on the plane's radio, asking for permission to take off. The tower instructed Fran to use the smaller airstrip. The pilots and mechanics in the area stopped what they were doing to watch.

After performing a final warmup, Fran rolled out onto the runway. Once the plane reached 90 miles an hour, she pulled up on the yoke and immediately felt the wheels leave the ground. She retracted the landing gear and headed off into the sky as dusk was falling. She could see the longer runway beneath her. They had aircraft lined across it, wing to wing, waiting for delivery. She figured that was the reason the tower had her use the shorter runway for takeoff.

As she flew from the runway, a white trailer on the edge of the base caught her eye. There was a flock of pigeons perched on the building's rooftop. She banked the plane away from the birds in case they decided to take flight. She could see stacks of birdcages surrounding the building and wondered if it was the pigeon training center Nancy had mentioned during her interview.

Fran flew to a remote area in the desert to perform a few maneuvers and get more familiar with the plane. She banked sharply to the right and into a roll. The plane's lightning fast response to any changes she made in flight astounded her.

It was February, and twilight came quickly. Remembering the fuel was low, she turned the plane to return to the base. However, when Fran got to where she thought the runways should be, she couldn't see them. There was only darkness where the base should have been. She called into the tower and glanced at the fuel gauge. The indicator pointed to empty.

"Hmm," Fran said to herself.

"Long Beach Tower," she said over the radio, "One-Five Victor inbound Two-Nine. Uh, where's the runway?"

"One-Five Victor, we hear you," the controller said. "Power is out. Keep flying until we can get you some lighting."

He told Fran that a recruit had accidentally backed a jeep into a utility pole while he was watching her take off. It had knocked out power for the entire base, including the landing lights for the runway.

"I've got General Pitts here," the controller said to Fran.

She heard the general's voice on the radio. "How's your fuel?" he asked.

"Minimum," she said, flying over the runway.

"I'm taking care of it," he said. "Hang in there."

After fifteen minutes passed, Fran could finally see the area below her. Jeeps had been lined up across from each other on both sides of the runway with their headlights turned on.

"One-Five Victor, cleared to land," the controller announced over the radio.

"Cleared to land, One-Five Victor," Fran repeated back. "From up here it doesn't look like there's enough space for the wings to clear the jeeps — they're too close."

"No time for go-arounds," the general said to her. "Come on, you got one shot at this — you can do it."

Fran lowered the plane's landing gear. As she turned onto final approach, she glanced nervously at the width of the runway between the jeeps. Suddenly, the engine stopped. Fran gasped. The plane had just run out of fuel.

"Here we go," she said, gritting her teeth.

The plane descended until its wheels touched down onto the dirt runway. Fran saw the wings of the P-39 come within inches of the jeeps parked on both sides of her. She pressed down on the brakes as the plane sped down the runway. When she turned to the left, the aircraft rolled to a stop. General Pitts jumped out of a jeep and ran down the runway towards her. When he got to the plane, Fran was climbing down the wing.

"Nice landing, Ace," he said, trying to catch his breath.

The other pilots, including John, watched quietly from the jeeps as she walked by.

"Thanks, guys!" Fran said with a wave.

A wolf whistle from one of the jeeps broke the silence. Fran knew it was CC. She could see Cornelia sitting beside her, grinning.

At that moment, Fran felt she could do anything; she was unstoppable. Not only did she fly airplanes for the army, but she also had these amazing women for friends. And they were a part of something that was making a difference.

CHAPTER 25

The next morning, Cornelia told Fran she'd overheard a conversation in the officers' club dining room about her P-39 flight.

"It sounds like you made the guys look bad," Cornelia chuckled.

"Well, maybe now they'll stop whining to General Pitts," Fran replied. "It's a dream of a plane, by the way. You should get certified in it."

"If they need me to, I will, but I'm happy flying any airplane. I feel good just knowing what I am doing is helping the war effort, and right now, it's the planes at the Vultee factory that need delivering. I'm heading there today to pick up another one. They're turning out so many of them we can't keep up."

After Cornelia left, Fran decided she would investigate the pigeon trailer she had seen the other night. She left their house and walked down the road to where she thought it could be. As she came closer, she could see a long building, mostly hidden by the surrounding trees. Its white paint appeared to be fresh, and like everything on the base, it looked recently constructed. Pigeons were perched on the building's flat roof, basking in the warmth of the sun. Small flaps were built on the sides of the building so the birds could also cool off inside. A young man in khakis and a white t-shirt stood in the doorway.

"Hello there," Fran said. "I noticed your place here with all the birds on the roof while I was out flying yesterday. I heard the army trains pigeons to deliver messages. Is that what these birds are for?"

"We don't train them here," he replied, "but these birds used to deliver messages. This is an aviary for the war veterans."

"These birds here have been out delivering messages in battle?" she asked.

"Yes, ma'am," he said. "They're trained homing pigeons that travel with the soldiers."

"Do they ever travel with pilots?"

"They sure do," he said. "When a plane crashes or has a radio failure, a pigeon can deliver a message with the location of the plane so a rescue mission can try to find the surviving crew. The pigeons also go in army tanks and battleships." He shaded his eyes from the sun to have a closer look at Fran. "Did you say you were a pilot? I thought you said you were flying over the aviary when you first saw it."

"Yes, I am," she said. "And I have a pigeon. I trained him to deliver messages."

"I'm Tom. I'm a pigeoneer." He lifted a large pail of grain and walked over to a nearby mobile coop hitched to a pickup truck. A pigeon flew off the roof and perched on his shoulder. "The building here is a breeding station. It's also gonna be a bird recovery hospital to patch up the wounded ones that make it back alive."

Tom told Fran the pigeoneers were a division of the U.S. Army Signal Corps that reported to Colonel Poutré, the chief pigeoneer. The colonel was stationed at their headquarters on the East Coast, where he trained pigeons to deliver messages.

Fran pointed to a sign hanging over the aviary's entrance that read "Joe's Pigeons."

"Who is Joe?"

Tom chuckled. "Oh, the sign, it's a joke. Joe is Sergeant McCormick. He's in charge of the aviary here at Long Beach. He's a legend. Joe — I mean, Sergeant McCormick. He trains recruits to care for their birds and treat their sicknesses and injuries. He also specializes in teaching the birds how to adjust to new locations, so they'll fly back to a different home base once they're out in the field. It's not easy — you see, pigeons tend to stick to one place as home base. The guys call the birds that Sergeant McCormick trains 'Joe's Pigeons.' His pigeons will fly across oceans into whiteout conditions. I've seen one that was attacked by a hawk but still made it back to deliver a message. Some pigeons are even awarded medals for their courage."

"Birds get medals?" Fran asked.

"Yep," Tom continued, "I heard of this one bird, Mocker, he flew fifty-two missions without getting wounded until this one mission when his eye and a chunk of his head got blown off by an explosion, but he still delivered his message about the enemy's location."

"Did he live?" she asked.

"Sure, he lived for a long while after that. He got a Dickin Medal for his bravery."

"Amazing. So, where's Sergeant McCormick?"

"He's at the naval base picking up Chickpea. She's one of our birds. The Nazis shot her while she was trying to deliver a message. She showed up with her leg hanging on by a tendon. The army medics saved her and carved her an artificial leg made of wood. He's picking her up. She can stay here and recover, maybe breed, if possible."

Fran thanked Tom and told him she'd stop back another day to meet the sergeant.

"Why not bring your bird next time?" he asked. "You can take some of our feed for your pigeon if you would like. And please do stop by again, ma'am."

When Fran returned to the barracks, she found CC crying alone in her room.

"What's wrong?" Fran asked.

"I got a telegram. Mikey's missing in action in Germany," she sobbed.

Fran held CC as she wept on her shoulder. Devastated, CC considered telling General Pitts that she was going to quit, but Fran convinced her to stay until March and complete the rest of the three months she'd committed to back in December. But CC, their great joke teller and kidder, was never to be the same.

CHAPTER 26

Two weeks after she flew the P-39, General Pitts summoned Frances to his office, along with CC, Nancy and Cornelia.

"It seems one of the boys spilled the beans about Project Peanut," he said. "Some loudmouth said something, and now the press has gotten wind of it."

The base on the East Coast had received a phone call concerning the rumor of a teenage girl landing a P-39 at an army base out in California. Charles Wheeler, a reporter for *The Boston Post*, had asked for confirmation that they were training women pilots to fly fighter planes. If it were true, he was hoping to take photos of them for a feature story. The office had transferred his call to General Pitts.

"Right up front," the general said, "I told him I didn't like the idea. I said my pilots are busy, and they don't have time for nonsense from the likes of you."

"Sounds like he wants a scoop," Nancy said. "Nobody knows about us yet."

"He asked if he could take a few photos and write a puff piece with a nice angle to it," General Pitts said. "Give citizens something positive to read about."

"You may as well let him," Fran said. "It'll eventually leak out to more newspapers, and we'll have reporters from *Life* magazine and even bigger newspapers than *The Boston Post* that'll push their way in. You can't stop the press."

"And that's a problem," he said. The general stood up from his desk and looked at the four of them. "I don't know how the American public is going to take this. I'd rather we focus on getting our mission accomplished instead of sensationalizing the fact that you are women."

When the reporter arrived at the base the next day, General Pitts escorted him to the area outside of the hangars, where the women were waiting for him. The general had let them know in advance that the reporter would want to take a few photos of them around the airplanes.

Fran watched the newsman step out of the jeep and then take his camera equipment out of the back. He looked young — maybe 18 — and stylishly dressed in pleated pants and a plaid suit jacket, his hair windblown from riding in the jeep.

"Look," Fran whispered, "he's just a baby, nothing to worry about."

He walked towards them with a slight limp in his step as the general drove off.

"Hi, there," he said. "Charles Wheeler. I'm a reporter for *The Boston...*" His voice trailed off.

"Lord have mercy," he said. "Nobody told me you were all so gorgeous."

The four women stared stonily at the young man.

Charles cleared his throat and looked over at a nearby plane. "Say, can you ladies pose for me around that aircraft right there?"

They all walked towards the mammoth-sized bomber plane.

"Can you really fly that?" he asked, pointing to a nearby pursuit plane.

Fran laughed. "I wouldn't ask that question around here if I were you."

A few of the mechanics came out from the hangar to watch the photoshoot.

"How about if one of you gets into that one?" he nodded at a P-39. "Any volunteers?" Nancy shrugged, then climbed up into the cockpit. Charles snapped a few photos with his Graflex press camera as she smiled graciously.

"Very nice," Charles said. "Thank you, ma'am."

"It's Nancy," she said.

"Thank you, Nancy."

The reporter had them pose in front of the bomber plane but didn't like how that looked. Instead, he had them walk towards him as he shot more photos.

"How long is this gonna take?" CC snapped.

She was impatient for the photo session to end because she didn't want to miss any news about Mikey. CC called the LA army base every day to ask if there was any news about her husband.

Charles took a notepad and a pencil from his shirt pocket.

"Can you each please spell out your first and last names for me?" he asked.

When Cornelia told him her name, he looked up. "You're that flight instructor that was at Pearl Harbor during the attack. I remember your name. You're the one that lived."

CC walked away, and the other three followed her.

"Uh, Frances," Charles stammered, "could I get a few more photos of you — maybe like standing here in front of the propeller?"

Cornelia nudged Fran as she walked past her. "He likes you," she whispered. Fran rolled her eyes and headed back over towards the plane's propeller.

She had noticed the reporter eyeing her earlier. Cornelia was right. Fran saw that familiar expression on his face, the one that looked like he was feeling ill. She knew it meant he found her attractive. She hadn't thought about dating again after her breakup, but there was an air about him, a self-confidence she felt drawn to. *I'll bet he lives in the city and has an exciting life.*

After taking a few photos, Charles thanked Fran, and she walked back with him to the general's office.

"Say, any chance I can buy you dinner tonight?" he asked. "That is if you don't have a boyfriend or a husband."

"Sure," Fran said. She knew she wasn't truly sure, but thought, why not? *Maybe this is how love works; you give someone a chance.*

"Great, I'll come back and pick you up at six then."

When she returned to the barracks, Cornelia was there, waiting.

"Hey, how about that reporter — did he ask you out?"

"He did. And I said yes. Even though I don't know why. He's not even my type at all."

"What is your type?"

Fran thought for a moment. "Someone...decent. You know, a guy with a kind soul. And tall and dashing doesn't hurt his chances, either. Take Gregory Peck, for example."

"So, if Greg asked you out, you would dump that poor reporter?" Cornelia teased. Fran nodded heartily, and they both laughed.

For her date, Fran wore her new navy dress and heels. She was also wearing makeup for the first time at the insistence of CC and Cornelia. They were both there to inspect her before she went out to meet Charles. She was wearing her mother's ring as her only jewelry.

"Try not to do anything scandalous," CC called out to her as she left.

Charles picked her up at six o'clock sharp in a rented convertible. His hair was slicked back, and he was wearing a Hawaiian shirt. A pack of cigarettes bulged from his front breast pocket, along with a pencil. Fran could see the muscles in his sinewy upper arms. When he saw her, he smiled devilishly.

"You look beautiful," he said, leaning over to push open the passenger door for her.

He drove out to a restaurant on the beach, and they found a table where they could watch the sunset. Surfers were in the water in front of the restaurant, riding their boards on the waves.

"Nice choice," Fran said, as he politely held her chair out for her.

"Yeah," Charles said, "the ocean here is something else — way better than the East Coast. Do you like seafood?" he asked as he looked over his menu.

"Yes."

"What do you think is good to order here on this side of the country?"

"So many things. I think the wild salmon, or the crab when it's in season."

Charles tapped his fingers on the table.

"What's it like in Boston?"

"Cold. I mean, freaking cold. Not as nice as the West Coast, that's for sure."

Fran liked the sound of his Boston accent.

A waitress with long blond hair came over to their table and took their order.

"I'll also have a beer," Charles said to the waitress. "Fran? Care for anything?"

She shook her head.

"I need to be awake early tomorrow. We fly out first thing in the morning."

The waitress left the two of them alone.

"It's pretty neat, you know. You being a pilot and all."

"I'm so happy to be getting to do this, to fly such magnificent machines — it's my dream come true. Do you enjoy working in the newspaper business?"

"It's okay. My boss is kind of a jerk. He screams at me a lot. He screams at everyone. It makes me nervous."

Charles took a cigarette out from the pack in his shirt pocket and offered her one. She shook her head.

"I'm trying to quit," he said, flipping open a Zippo to light his cigarette. "The *Post* is a good paper, but it's all just so negative. News that is. My first day on the job was Pearl Harbor. I mean, how crazy is that? Do you know what they say in the newsroom? If it bleeds, it leads." He took a drag of his cigarette.

"Most news seems to be about something bad that happened," Fran said. "My younger brother works for the paper out in Oregon. He loves the news business. He wants to work as a reporter."

The server brought them their food, and they ate in silence as they admired the sun setting over the ocean. Fran glanced over at Charles a few times during dinner and caught him staring at her. She snuck a few glances at him, but she didn't think he noticed.

"Is there something else you've always wanted to do instead of reporting?" Fran asked.

"Not really. Well, sort of. I used to box. You know, in the ring. I was pretty good, I guess. Last summer, while I was working at the paper in the printing room, an ink drum broke loose and rolled over on my leg and crushed it. I was in the hospital for four months."

"That's horrible. Can you still box?"

"Nah, I can't go in the ring, but I still work out at the gym. I like to watch fights. Anyway, my editor lets me help cover the fights. I don't get to take photos, just bring the photographer's film back to the newsroom. I wish I could interview the fighters. Maybe someday. That's my dream."

"Try to imagine yourself interviewing fighters. You can do it before you fall asleep. That's the best time. We're always imagining something in our heads, may as well be something you want to have happen."

"Yeah, I guess I'll try that. It wouldn't hurt. Now, if I could only get an incredible photo, I could write my ticket. At least that's what my editor says. He says I need to pull my socks up, whatever that means. I'm trying to get a job at the *LA Times*. We'll see if they hire me. I'm keeping my fingers crossed. If they don't, I'm afraid I'll get stuck with some crummy war correspondent assignment."

Fran felt a wave of overwhelming grief come over her. *Danny.* She sighed a deep sigh. She'd been so busy that she hadn't thought about her twin in a long time. It caught her off guard.

"Try not thinking about negative outcomes," she told him. "My parents are negative thinkers. I know it's tough to learn how to think differently, but it's possible."

Danny could do it. He was always positive.

"What do your folks think about you being a pilot for the army?"

"Well, they don't know about it. But my father will disown me when he finds out, and I am pretty sure that's going to happen once he sees your story. My mother left, and we haven't heard from her since. That was in June."

"That's tough. Mine died in a car crash when I was a baby. My grandparents raised me, so I don't remember them — my parents, that is."

"You've done well for yourself. They'd be proud of you."

Charles smiled at the thought as he sipped his beer.

"This feature with you and the other female pilots," he said, "I got a feeling that readers are going to go nuts about it. I have this extra sense for finding a good story. I have what they call in the business 'a nose for news.'"

As they were driving back to the base, Fran realized she liked Charles. She found him easy to talk to and ambitious, but she still hopped out of the car as soon as it stopped. He jumped out quickly as well and stood next to her, then slid in closer to kiss her. Before he could, she pressed her hand up against his chest and held him back. She could feel his heart racing. Fran felt his muscles flex under his shirt as he leaned in closer. She almost relaxed her hand but enjoyed being in control. She also felt excited — or maybe frightened. Fran had never felt that with John.

"Thank you for dinner," she said. Charles relaxed and leaned back against the car door.

"My pleasure," he said in a low voice. He smiled a sly grin and lowered his eyes. "I'd love to see you again."

She smiled but didn't answer him.

Cornelia was waiting to pounce as soon as Fran came into the barracks.

"Well, how did it go?" she asked. "Do you like him?"

Fran flopped down on her bed.

"Yes."

"Did he try to get fresh?"

"He tried, but I didn't let him. But if he asks me out again, well, I just might."

"Fran Finkel! Really now."

Wheeler's women pilots feature only made it to the Boston newspaper's second page, but the press saw it. Soon after that, the Long Beach base was buzzing with magazine and newspaper reporters who wanted photos and interviews, as Fran had predicted. The press exaggerated in their stories about the women pilots and even made some up.

But one thing was true: Project Peanut was no longer a secret.

CHAPTER 27

During the next few weeks, Fran kept busy learning everything she could about the type of bomber planes she had once followed into Pendleton. She had wished she could fly the B-25s then, and now she was being trained to do just that.

She found the aircraft's performance incredible for such a large ship. After several weeks of training, she completed the required hours of cross-country with an instructor. Soon after that, she passed her check-ride with flying colors.

Fran, CC and Nancy were all quickly certified to ferry B-25 bomber planes along with the men. Cornelia was too busy delivering planes from the Vultee factory to train to fly bombers or pursuit planes.

Once the pilots began delivering planes all over the country, they saw little of each other. Sometimes they didn't have time to sleep or eat. They were lucky if they got to stay overnight and clean up before their next assignment.

On a rare night that Fran, CC and Cornelia happened to all be at their Long Beach house, the phone rang. CC ran to get it, hoping it was news about Mikey.

It was Charles calling for Fran.

"I can't stop thinking about you," the reporter said. "What have you been up to?"

"Uh," CC told him, "I think you're looking for someone else, buddy."

She called out for Fran. Once she was on the line, Charles flirted shamelessly with her. Fran found him charming and felt excited at the thought of seeing the young reporter again.

"CC, do you think I could borrow your red dress?" Fran asked after her call with Charles ended.

"Sure, but why?" CC asked with raised eyebrows.

"Charles asked if he could see me again and if I could wear something extra nice. I think he's planning on taking me somewhere fancy, and I don't have any fancy dresses besides my blue one, and I already wore it to our first date."

"Sure, you can borrow it. Just be careful. I don't know if I trust that guy. He seems like a smooth talker. Take it slow."

CC left the room to get her dress for Fran.

"So, are you thinking this is serious?" Cornelia asked. "Maybe boyfriend material?"

Fran wasn't sure, but she felt attracted to him.

"He's trying to get a job in LA," she told Cornelia. "I guess we'll see."

She winked and raised her voice so CC could hear her in the other room. "If we were to get married, at least I'd live in a big city with jazz, wonderful restaurants, and dancing and that sort of thing."

"Married!" CC said, rushing back to their room. "Whoa, what'd I just say about taking it slow?"

Fran and Cornelia both laughed.

When Charles arrived, he waited for Fran to meet him out past the guard shack near the hangars.

"You look dazzling," he told her as he stepped out of the car. He grabbed his camera from the back seat.

"Hey, what's that for?" she asked.

"I figured since you looked so nice, why waste it? Let me take a few photos of you by one of the planes."

"I guess," Fran said. She eyed him suspiciously. "I thought we were going out for dinner?"

He leaned in to kiss her, but Fran backed away. "Don't you need permission from General Pitts to come out here?" she asked.

"Ah, yes, of course. I will if we get any good shots but let me shoot now before I lose this great lighting."

He began explaining his intentions as they walked towards one of the planes.

"You see, my first female pilot story only made it to the *Post's* second page. My boss said it was boring. I said to him, 'Boring? It's women pilots. What's boring about that?' He said, 'The photos are boring, why would I care? Why do I want to read this? Wheeler, if you want a story to go national, then you need to seduce the reader with your photos.'"

Charles gestured for Fran to stand in front of a nearby plane. Once she did, he started snapping photos of her.

"Great, that's beautiful. Very sexy." He stopped shooting and looked up and over the aircraft.

"Why don't you climb up on the wing and pretend to be stepping into the cockpit? That way, I can see a little more leg."

"In a dress, are you serious? Charles, I'm wearing heels. Call me crazy, but it seems a little out of place."

"Yeah, I suppose you're right. It would make a good shot, though. Say, you don't have a bathing suit by any chance, do you?"

"A bathing suit?!"

"Yeah, I think that would be perfect. The more skin, the better!"

"Are you serious? Is that why you asked me out — so I could be a pinup girl in some stupid shop calendar?"

"Say, that's not stupid at all. People would love that. I was thinking of the front page of newspapers, but that's an even better idea!"

"I would never pose for something like that! It's not who I am," Fran said, marching away from the plane. "Goodnight, Mr. Wheeler."

"Suit yourself, but one day you'll be sorry!" Charles called after her. "There's a girl working in an airplane factory in Burbank — name's Norma Jeane. She's real sexy. I know she'll let me take her picture. Mark my words, she's going to be a star!"

Fran stormed back home to the barracks.

"I hate reporters!" she cried out in disgust as she slammed the door.

Before Charles had the opportunity to take photos of Norma Jeane, an army photographer was given the assignment. A modeling agency saw her pictures in the newspaper and offered her a contract. She accepted it and later signed on with a movie studio that changed her name to Marilyn Monroe.

CHAPTER 28

Soon after her fiasco with Charles, the general added Fran to the schedule to deliver her first B-25, which meant she would finally have the chance to ferry one of the big ships. In the meantime, she had let the thought of the Boston reporter become nothing but a memory. Only now, she had become enamored with the notion of meeting Joe, the legendary pigeoneer.

On the first day Fran didn't have to attend training, she brought Easter with her to the aviary, hoping the sergeant would be there. When she arrived, she let Easter free. He flew onto the rooftop with the other birds as Tom was stepping out of the aviary.

"Wow," he said when he saw Easter. "What a beautiful bird! I've never seen one with those markings."

"That's Easter," she told him.

"That's Blackie next to Easter," Tom said, pointing to the row of birds on the rooftop, "and Holy Ghost, G.I. Jane, Willie, Monkey, Pork Chop and Cracker Jack. All the birds have their own serial number so the army can keep track of them, but Sergeant McCormick names them as well."

Easter stretched his wings and flew over towards Fran and Tom.

"Is Easter fast? He looks like he's built for speed."

"Yes, he can clock seventy miles an hour, over a mile a minute."

"No way! That's the fastest I've ever heard!"

"Is Sergeant McCormick here today?"

Tom rubbed his short haircut. "No, ma'am. You just missed him."

"You know, I'm starting to wonder if he exists," she teased.

"He does so! That's his desk and office, right in there. Have a look for yourself." Tom pointed to a doorway at the end of the aviary.

Fran walked into the sergeant's office. Besides a desk and two chairs, the inside of the office was barren. There were several framed photos of birds hanging on the wall. When Fran looked closer, she noticed a newspaper clipping pinned to a cluttered bulletin board. In the article was a photo of a pigeon that resembled Easter.

The caption below the photo read:

"Martha is the last known passenger pigeon in the world. A $25,000 reward will be offered for anyone who discovers another in existence."

The accompanying article said the aviary's supervisor, Joe McCormick, was now working for the Army Air Corps pigeoneer squadron. Anyone with information about a passenger pigeon should contact the Chicago Zoo.

Tom walked up and stood behind her as she was reading the clipping and chuckled.

"You know," he said, "most guys pin up a photo of their girlfriend. He's the only guy I know who pins up a picture of a bird. He's something else, that's for sure. Like, he's been training the birds to fly at night. It's against their nature. And he's been quite successful. You see, the enemy would shoot a pigeon just in case it was carrying a message — then you're out of luck — but they can't see them if it's dark."

"That is rather remarkable," Fran said. "I'd love to meet him. I promise I'll come back and try to catch Sergeant McCormick another time."

When Fran returned to the barracks, she told CC about the reward and the sergeant.

"I'm not so sure about this sergeant," CC said. "That's a lot of money for a bird. What if he tries to steal Easter from you?"

"Or maybe he's wonderful," Fran said, "and everything Tom says about him is true."

CC promised she'd do some snooping around. If Fran's bird was indeed a passenger pigeon, she wasn't sure he was someone they could trust with the knowledge of Easter. Their conversation about the mystery of the passenger pigeon was cut short when General Pitts called the women's barracks, asking for Fran.

The general told her he'd received a call from a studio producer in Hollywood who asked if he could film one of their Twin Beech transport airplanes for a movie he was shooting in Burbank.

"Seems you're scheduled to pick up a B-25 on Friday," he said. "But you're also certified to fly transport planes, including the Beech that the producer wants. I figured you're the least likely to get caught up in the Hollywood scene or even interested in it. Out of the pilots that can fly transport planes, you are my most disciplined — and possibly my best — pilot on staff. I need someone who can serve as a representative of my hard-working team of pilots."

Fran smiled. Inside, she was bursting with pride.

"Why didn't you ask Nancy?" she asked.

"I did. She said no way. She hates that flashy Hollywood scene."

Fran considered Nancy's response and hesitated at first. However, the general was entrusting her with his teams' reputation, and she didn't want to let him down.

"If you can get back here tomorrow, I'll get you on a transport plane with Snafu airlines. That'll get you to your B-25 in plenty of time, and you won't have to take the bus."

"That would be fantastic," Fran said. "Thank you, sir."

"There's going to be lots of reporters floating around," he told her, "since it's always swarming with movie stars out there, so make sure you keep a low profile. As you know, Project Peanut has had some bad press. Newspaper reporters are making up stories, and we don't need to give them any more feed for their newsreels. Got it?"

"Sure. I'll keep a low profile. Should I wear my uniform?" Fran asked.

"Yes, you should. You are a pilot who flies for the army, but we don't want reporters putting a spotlight on that. Not right now. Let their stories die down like they always do."

"Yes, sir."

"I should never have let that Boston kid in here. Avoid the press and if you see them, run in the other direction."

After she checked out the Beech and was taxiing for takeoff, Fran saw General Pitts waving by the runway to get her attention. He made a hand gesture to imply keeping a low profile. She smiled and nodded.

"Yeah," she muttered under her breath, "I get it."

The trip was a brief hop. In less than an hour, she landed at the Lockheed Airport in Burbank, where the producer wanted to shoot b-roll of the plane for his film. A car was waiting there for her. The driver took her to the Ambassador Hotel, where Fran checked into a complimentary room, paid for by the producer.

She went to her room, changed out of her flight suit and into her uniform, and then went downstairs to look for the dining room. She walked by a large room filled with people dressed in evening gowns and tuxedos. It was the hotel's lounge. Benny Goodman's band was playing on the stage. Fran recognized the tune they were playing; it brought back memories of her dance lessons. It was one of her mother's favorite songs, and for a fleeting moment, Fran realized she missed her. The feeling took her by surprise.

When she saw how packed the dining room was, she opted to have dinner at the bar. As Fran was looking over the menu, she recognized a familiar voice.

"Bartender, can I get a beer, please?"

Fran hid behind her menu when she heard that Boston accent. She peered out, then ducked back behind the menu as the bartender brought him a beer.

She couldn't believe it. Charles, of all people. *What were the odds?*

"I got myself an interview with Barney Ross, the professional boxing triple champion," she overheard him say to the bartender. "He's won world titles in three weight divisions. This guy's my idol."

Charles waved to a muscular, middle-aged man walking towards the bar with a cane. He had a youthful grin with a gap between his two front teeth, while his hair had gone completely gray. Fran wondered if he had experienced something horrible to cause it.

"Mr. Ross, over here!" Charles shouted at him as the fighter made his way to the bar.

"Sir, it is such a thrill meeting you," Charles said, holding out his hand. "Thank you so much for taking the time for an interview tonight. I know you're a busy man."

"No problem, Charles," he said, shaking the reporter's hand. "So, you said you boxed?"

Charles nodded. "I was pretty good, that is, before my leg injury."

Fran listened to their conversation, hoping for some distraction so she could escape without Charles spotting her.

"Your last fight with Henry Armstrong was one of the most brutal fights I ever saw," Charles said. "You should have let them take you out. What made you stay? Why not let them stop the fight? You weren't going to win."

He didn't answer Charles. The bartender brought a beer over for the champion.

"Mr. Ross," Charles asked, "what is it that makes you so unstoppable?"

"Because I believe, that's what. I know I can overcome anything."

His answer intrigued Fran. She wondered if he had always had that amount of faith in himself.

"I was just a kid when robbers shot and killed my father. I grew up angry after that happened. Some people say it's the hate that drives me, but that's not it. I don't waste my energy on hate. It's love for my family that inspires me."

Mr. Ross drank his beer while Charles took notes.

"After the Pearl Harbor bombing," he continued, "I enlisted. Nobody else in my family could, and I wanted to serve this country that let me, a runt kid from Chicago's ghetto, become a champion. Hitler may kill millions of us Jews, but he needs to know what he's up against. He'll never defeat us."

"I heard you single-handedly killed twenty-two of the enemy with four hundred rounds and twenty-two grenades," Charles said.

"Meh," the fighter shrugged. "I needed a good workout so I could get back in the ring," he joked. "Charles, why don't you consider becoming a war correspondent. You know, go overseas?"

"Excuse me," Charles said, avoiding his question. "I'd love to get a photo for my story, but I left my camera in the car. Mind if I go get it?"

Mr. Ross gestured for him to leave.

After Charles was out of sight, Fran took her opportunity and fled from the bar. She headed over to the lounge, figuring she could slip in and sit at an empty table way in the back. It was dark inside, and nobody would notice her.

Once inside the nightclub, her eyes adjusted to the darkness as she looked around at the crowd. At first, Fran thought it couldn't be true, but the woman sitting at one of the round tables near the band appeared to be Ingrid Bergman, the movie star. And she was speaking to a man who looked exactly like Gary Cooper.

A waiter in a white suit and black tie came to Fran's table and placed a glass of champagne in front of her.

"I'm sorry," Fran said, "I didn't order that."

"Compliments of the club's owner, miss."

She gasped at the surprise. "Oh my, well, in that case, please tell the owner I said thank you." She smiled at the server and then took a sip of champagne.

"Say," Fran said in a low voice, "is that Ingrid Bergman there, in the front?"

The waiter looked over and nodded. "Yes. She's one of our regulars. Many movie stars frequent our club."

A small dance floor was in front of the band, and a few couples were out dancing to the music. Fran smiled, remembering the dances she had gone to in high school with John. She sighed.

That's definitely Ginger Rogers dancing.

Fran recognized even more stars: Bob Hope, Kate Hepburn and Spencer Tracy.

Everyone in here is famous.

It was all like a dream until the music stopped, and a balding man stepped up onto the stage.

"Ladies and gentlemen," he proclaimed. "Thank you for coming out here to the Cocoanut Grove tonight to be our guests. And in case you haven't noticed yet, we are being honored by the presence of a special guest. There is a United States Army pilot in our audience right now."

Fran was looking around the room like everyone else until she was blinded by a bright spotlight aimed at her. She could hear people in the room talking and the band playing a fanfare.

"It's one of those women pilots!" she heard someone in the crowd cry out.

People began applauding. Someone even whistled a wolf whistle. She squinted as her vision returned. Movie stars were everywhere, all of them clapping and standing up. For her.

Blushing, she stood, took a bow and waved.

Fran prayed silently. *Please don't let there be any press in here.* The din from the crowd grew even louder. Finally, everyone sat back down. The spotlight moved away from her and back to the band.

Fran could see someone gliding towards her. A tall, slender figure wearing a tuxedo. The band started playing her favorite song, "A Nightingale Sang in Berkeley Square."

"Excuse me," the tall figure said with a dazzling smile. "I see that perhaps you may be the only person here who is younger than me. Allow me to introduce myself."

But Fran didn't need his introduction. She knew who he was.

"Name's Greg," he continued, "Greg Peck. Would you care to dance?" He held out his hand as he invited her to the dance floor. Fran just stood there in a dazed shock.

"I would consider it an honor," he said in a deep voice.

For the first time in her life, Fran was grateful for those years of dance lessons her mother had given her.

She took his hand. And at that moment, she heard the pop of a flashbulb.

After dancing all night with the dashing movie star, Fran went back to her room. She'd always dreamed of meeting Greg, and now her dream had come true. Only now was an awful time for it to happen.

It seems the Universe doesn't have the timing right for getting what you want. Sometimes by the time it happens, you may not want it anymore. It could even be a bad thing.

She had heard the flashbulb and figured it was Charles. *Maybe the photo won't come out. Perhaps the paper doesn't care about Gregory Peck and me. General Pitts probably won't read The Boston Post.* These thoughts were the positive ones she was using to fight against the negative ones that repeated in her mind: *I screwed up. The general is going to throw me out, and I will never have the chance to fly a B-25 ever again.*

CHAPTER 29

The same driver brought Fran back to the airport early the following day. After returning to the base, she went straight to the room she shared with Cornelia and began packing her travel bag. She knew she'd get to Dallas early if she left now, but she didn't care. She was hurrying to pick up the B-25 when Nancy walked into her room.

"Did you see the Sunday paper today?" she asked Fran.

"Uh, no. I was in Hollywood. I just got here."

"I know." She tossed a newspaper onto Fran's bunk. "Everyone in the country knows you were in Hollywood last night."

On the front page of the *LA Times* was a photo of an attractive young woman in an army pilot's uniform, smiling at Gregory Peck. He was holding her hand up to his face, admiring her ring. The headline read: "Female Army Pilot Enchants Movie Star."

Fran stared at the paper in amazement.

"Is that me?" she asked.

"It certainly bears a strong resemblance, wouldn't you say?" Nancy answered.

"Is Finkel back yet?!" General Pitts shouted as he walked into their barracks. He pointed his finger at her. "You," he said. "You come with me. We need to talk."

When they got into his office, there was a stack of newspapers sprawled across his desk. His phone was ringing, and he picked it up.

"Hello?" he said into the receiver. "No, Miss Finkel isn't doing any interviews." The general put the receiver down and groaned. He gestured for her to sit, then pointed to the newspaper opened on his desk.

"Nice photo," General Pitts said. "What happened to our low-pro-file plan?"

He had sent her there to be their representative. And she had let him down. She failed. Fran went into a cold sweat as she began to feel ill.

"I said, LOW PROFILE!"

He slammed his fist down on the desk.

Fran squirmed in her chair, wishing she could disappear.

The general sighed. "You got picked up — your photo, that is. It went national. All the big papers are running it. *LA Times, The New York Post, The Washington Post, The Chicago Tribune*, all front-page news."

Papa and Seamus will see it, too, Fran thought. Then they'll know. Maybe even mother will. Fran was proud to be flying planes for the army but wondered how they would feel about it.

"Finkel, listen to me!" the general barked. "I need this reporter feeding frenzy to stop. The folks in Washington will see this, including members of Congress who are voting next week to decide whether to let women pilots in the army with full benefits. Surely this will not lean the vote in your favor, by the way."

The next day, General Pitts and Nancy learned Congress was considering ending Project Peanut because of the negative press. They decided it would be best to go to Washington right away to persuade public officials to allow the program to continue.

Time was precious. The general asked for a volunteer to fly them to Washington in one of the army transport planes so they could prepare for the meeting during the flight. It wasn't a favorite job — ferrying new planes was preferable. Hoping to get back in his good graces, Fran offered to take them, knowing it also meant she would have to let another ferry pilot take her first B-25 assignment.

The three of them flew out of the Long Beach airport early the next morning. When they were about 1,200 miles from Washington's National Airport, Fran landed to refuel. Nancy was in the copilot seat writing notes. General Pitts was in the back of the plane, preparing what he would say at the meeting. When Fran taxied to the fuel center, the attendant told her they were out of gas. She took off and flew to the nearest airport, only they were also out of fuel.

That's when General Pitts came up from the back of the plane to the cockpit.

"What's the problem?" he asked.

"Nobody has fuel," Nancy told him.

"There's an airport in Southern Iowa, about one hundred miles from here," General Pitts told her. "It's for authorized military use only, but we should be fine to land. Do we have enough fuel to make it there?"

Fran sighed and nodded once.

"Then leave now and make it snappy," he said as he climbed into the back of the plane. "I don't want to be late."

Fran turned to a northerly heading that would bring them to the military airport.

"Wow," Nancy said, "he's furious. I hope that dance was worth it."

As soon as Fran landed on the runway, jeeps approached the plane to escort them down the airstrip. At first, Fran thought they were being respectful, until she saw soldiers riding in back, aiming rifles at them. One of the jeeps pulled up on their left. Fran taxied off the runway towards the fuel station, and the jeep continued to drive along beside them.

After they had stopped, General Pitts pushed open the exit in the back of the plane and walked down the steps.

"What the hell is going on here?!" he shouted.

"You need to leave," the young officer driving the jeep told him. "You're not authorized to be here. My orders are to keep this area free of unauthorized airplanes."

General Pitts took a deep breath.

"I admire your dedication to your post, private," he said to the young officer. "I am Lieutenant General William Pitts, the commanding officer of the Army Air Force Air Transport Command's ferrying division. We need fuel. We're scheduled to meet with Congress, and I don't want us to be late. I promise you we'll be quickly on our way after we refuel."

The young man pointed at the fuel attendants and gestured for them to fill the plane. General Pitts thanked him. The young man saluted. When the general climbed back inside the aircraft, he didn't say a word to Fran or Nancy.

"It's not only your photo, Fran," Nancy told her. "Project Peanut's taking a lot of heat from all the bad press. There have been complaints that we're taking all the good jobs away from the men while we live a glamorous lifestyle, which you know is ridiculous. That's what this meeting is about. The general's worried they'll shut us down, and that will impact our plane delivery schedule. It may even cause another backlog."

Fran couldn't believe what was happening. Sure, she wanted to be famous, but not for this. Aviation historians would discover female pilots were never allowed in the military because some foolish girl pilot danced with a movie star.

Fortunately, General Pitts and Nancy were able to convince the lawmakers to postpone ending Project Peanut until they met for their next session. This would delay voting on the bill to let women pilots fly for the army. It wasn't ideal, but it bought them some time.

CHAPTER 30

Exhausted, Fran stepped off the bus that dropped her off at the base in Long Beach. It was a late Thursday evening in March. She had been delivering pursuit planes for ten days straight and was looking forward to going to bed. When she arrived at the women's barracks, she sighed.

Fran put down her travel bag and took Easter out of her flight suit pocket where the bird was sleeping. When she caught a glimpse of herself in the mirror, her appearance took her by surprise.

"Wow, I really look like a boy," she said to her reflection. Her cropped hair was unruly from the humidity.

After having her photo on the front page of the most read newspapers in the nation, Fran discovered she couldn't go anywhere without someone recognizing her. And everyone had an opinion; some people adored her, while others thought she was a disgrace. Worried she'd wind up on the front pages again, she went to a hairdresser before her 10-day jaunt and had her hair cut short to pass for a boy. Although it wouldn't help much when she was wearing a dress, she had hoped it would keep down the attention.

And it worked. After that, people didn't even notice her when she traveled, and she wasn't in the newspaper again.

She glanced over at her bed and noticed that Cornelia had left her a letter. The two had started leaving each other notes with an update whenever one of them returned to the base. Most of the time, it was the only communication they had. Any correspondence from her comrade meant a lot to Fran.

"My dear friend, not much new to report. Yes, I am still delivering the trainers, I know, I know. Are you as exhausted as I am from all this travel? I'm hoping to get back to our home base on Friday. I heard you got a haircut. Really? — C."

"She needs to get checked out to fly bigger planes," Fran said to herself as she flopped onto her bed. The jolt caused her thought book to fall to the floor. She realized it had been some time since she focused on what she wanted. Fran began to wonder what that was now.

She had committed to ferrying for three months. The time had passed so quickly. After all the press trouble, Fran wondered if General Pitts would say he didn't need her anymore once her three months ended. She sighed at the memory of her dance with Greg. As she drifted off to sleep, Fran imagined meeting someone like him one day — someone kind. And falling in love.

That night, Fran dreamt she was flying in formation with six other pilots when she crashed into one of the other planes.

"Don't do it, Frankie," she heard Danny say. She felt herself falling and woke up with a start. She sat up in her bed, soaked in sweat.

Nervous about being let go after her commitment had ended, Fran went to General Pitts' office early that morning to look at the delivery schedule. When she didn't see her name on the assignment board for the entire week, it made Fran even more worried that the general was going to tell her he would no longer need her once her three months were up. The ferry pilots had caught up on the backlog of planes at factories on the West Coast and were seeing a lull in the number of assignments. Several of the pilots were allowed to take leave and visit their families. She wondered if she could figure out how to see Seamus, since her father had told her that if she left, she shouldn't come back.

When she returned to the barracks, CC was in her room, packing her travel bag. Fran plopped down on one of the bunk beds.

"What happened to your hair?" she asked when she saw Fran.

"It's easier this way. You know — less maintenance." She didn't want to get into the real reason.

"It's cute. Say, kiddo, I went back to the aviary while you were away to see if that Sergeant Joe fella was around. You know, to sniff him out and see if I could learn anything about the last passenger pigeon. And he was there."

"Did you find anything out?" Fran asked.

"I did."

CC sat down beside her on the bed.

"His father is some big shot director at the Chicago Zoo. He spends most of his time organizing fundraisers and finding rich guys to make donations. He got Joe a job working in the aviary. That passenger pigeon you saw in the newspaper clipping is his favorite bird. She's been there as long as he can remember. You should hear him go on about that bird. I swear he was getting all choked up." She rolled her eyes as she continued packing. "He feels sorry for her because she's all alone and also because she's the only one in existence, so it's a big deal at the zoo.

People always want to see her. Visitors used to throw sand at her cage to get her to move, so he put a fence around her area so they couldn't."

"People are terrible," Fran said.

"You should go meet him," CC said, "I think you'd like him."

"Oy vey," Fran said and waved her off. "What, exactly, is so special about this mysterious pigeon guy, anyway?"

"I don't know," CC said. She stopped packing and smiled. "There's just something about him. I can feel he's a kind soul. Anyway, at least bring Easter over there, for goodness' sake, so you can collect that reward. Besides, you'll make his day. Those birds are incredible. Maybe I'll get one to fly with me while I look for Mikey."

"What do you mean, 'while you look for Mikey'?"

Cornelia walked into the room, wearing her flight suit and carrying her travel bag and parachute.

"Hey, ladies!" she said. "On my way over, I stopped to see the schedule. Looks like neither of you is on it. Why's that? We're delivering some trainers to Texas this Sunday and could use another pilot. Sorenson, your ex, is one of the regular guys assigned to deliver trainers, but he just went on leave to get married."

"You want to go?" Fran asked CC.

"Nope. I'm through."

"What?!"

"I quit today."

"You can't!" Cornelia cried. "CC, no!"

"Well, I can't do this anymore. My heart's not in it. I need to do what I can to help find my husband, you know?"

There was a sadness in CC's eyes that wasn't there when they first met. Fran had seen it in her parents' eyes; it happened after losing a loved one.

CC needed some closure, but she didn't know how to find it. Fran didn't, either. *Maybe nobody does.*

"I'll go," Fran said, "but only if it's okay with General Pitts."

Late that afternoon, Fran felt the urge to walk on the beach. She missed the ocean and felt homesick. She asked Cornelia to come with her for a walk. After dinner, they drove out to the coast.

On their walk, Fran asked her about Pearl Harbor.

"It was the most frightening time I have ever had flying," Cornelia told her. "The owner of the flight school I worked for was killed. I had been talking to him earlier that morning. I still can't believe he's gone, you know? It's like, you never know when it's the last time you'll talk to someone in this life."

They walked together in silence, with only the sound of the waves crashing on the shore.

"I had told you I only had one brother," Fran said. "But I used to have two. I've never told anyone this before. My twin brother, Danny, was carried off by a wave when he tried to save our dog. I saw it happen. I was there."

"Fran, I'm so sorry. I have brothers, and I can't imagine losing one."

"We fought all the time, but he was my best friend. I mean, we learned to fly together. He was someone I could talk to about anything, you know, like you."

After sharing her secret with Cornelia, they both sat down near the shore. Fran wept in silence as they looked out at the ocean.

"I worry about my little brother, Seamus," Fran said. "Gosh, I send him letters all the time. I wonder if my father isn't letting him see them or if he hates me because I left."

"How about we ask the general for a leave, and we go visit him?" Cornelia said, and squeezed Fran's shoulder.

"I would like that. Papa will be angry, but at least I can see my brother again. I miss him so much."

CHAPTER 31

Fran was tidying up her room Saturday afternoon when General Pitts called her to his office for the first time since the photo fiasco.

"Nice haircut," he said curtly.

She rolled her eyes.

"I'm going to need you to help deliver trainers for a while. I'm short a ferry pilot. Once he's back from his honeymoon, I'll see about getting you assigned back to the big planes again." He told Fran she would be on the schedule to ferry Valiants starting Sunday.

That evening, Fran, Cornelia and the other four male pilots scheduled to go to the Vultee factory sat together at the same table in the officers' club. They decided over dinner to meet outside of the barracks at dawn to pick up the planes.

Early the next morning, they all climbed into the back of an army jeep headed for the airplane factory. It was misty when they left the base, but the fog had burned off by the time they arrived. They completed the required paperwork for each plane and then headed outside to check out their aircraft.

Six blue and yellow trainer planes were waiting for them outside in the sunshine. Each pilot chose a plane and went through their checklist. After Fran climbed into the cockpit of her plane, the memory of her dream came back. She felt a cold chill run down her spine. Cornelia must have noticed something was wrong because she walked over to check on her.

"You okay?" she asked. "You look like you've seen a ghost."

"I feel spooked about a dream I had the other night. I don't think we should go."

"What? Fran, we can't just leave the planes here. We already filled out the paperwork. Now we have to deliver them."

Cornelia walked back to her plane to finish her checklist. Fran sat still in her plane's cockpit as she wrestled with what to do.

She figured General Pitts would send her home if she left without the aircraft, which meant she would never fly a B-25. As she watched the others preparing for their flight, she wondered if it was possible to change her future with thoughts. *Can positive affirmations stop something from happening? Can thoughts change an outcome?*

Fran climbed out of the cockpit and went through her checklist again to make sure she hadn't missed anything. The other pilots had already left. She jumped back into the plane and looked around.

"Clear!" she shouted as she started the engine. The propeller spun slowly. Her stomach lurched as she taxied towards the airstrip.

"Everything is going to be just fine," she told herself halfheartedly. She turned on the radio and announced her airplane's call sign with the intention to takeoff. After she was airborne, Fran quickly caught up with the other pilots.

Although it had been a while, Fran had made this trip dozens of times when she first started ferrying planes. Finally, she began to relax. *Cornelia's right — I have to do this. It's why we're here. I can't let the general down.*

Once they were away from the populated areas, Fran could see three planes flying in close formation ahead of her.

"I'll be the flight leader," she heard one of them say over the radio. "I'm first on the left, then Jones, Harrington, Maloney and Fort. Finkel, you'll be on the right end."

Fran watched as another pilot slid in to join the formation. Now four planes were flying beside each other with only a few feet between each of their wingtips.

"I don't want any part of this," Fran replied over the radio.

"I'm out, too," one of the male pilots said. He left the formation to fly in front of the others.

Fran drew in her breath and stayed back about a quarter of a mile from the other pilots. She shook her head when Cornelia joined the formation, remembering what Nancy had told them. Now Cornelia's plane was the last one on the right.

When Fran saw Cornelia's plane suddenly snap roll to the right of the formation, she assumed she had decided to leave the group.

"Good girl," Fran said. But when Cornelia's plane went into a spin, she knew something must have gone wrong.

"Release the hatch, Cornelia!" Fran shouted. "Get out! Jump! Come on!"

Fran waited, expecting to see a parachute open below her.

"What just happened?" she asked on the radio.

"Don't know," one of the pilots responded. "I think I bumped her plane. I'm gonna try to land — I may have busted my landing gear."

Fran banked a 180-degree turn to go back and circle the area.

"Try to make it to the nearest airport and call this in ASAP!" she commanded. "I'm going to land and try to find her."

CHAPTER 32

After circling the nearby desert area below, Fran found a flat place to land and climbed out of her plane. She walked for over an hour in the stifling heat, still wearing her parachute pack, until she came upon a small hill. Sweaty and dust-covered, Fran climbed it to have a better view. As she scanned the horizon, she noticed a large tree and near it, an object that looked like Cornelia's plane, hidden by a pile of branches.

As Fran approached the location, she could see that it was a plane. Its nose buried several feet into the earth. Fran saw Cornelia slumped over inside the hatch. She wasn't moving.

"No, no, no, this isn't happening," Fran said. Dropping to her knees, she put her hand against the side of the plane.

"Please, please, let this be a dream. I'm dreaming, right?"

She looked up at the sky and stood up, shaking her fist. "How can you be so terrible!" she screamed. "First Danny and now her? Why do you need the good ones?"

She could hear police sirens in the distance. They were growing louder. They were coming closer.

Fran began to sob.

Not this. Not again.

She felt as if a dam in her mind had broken. Forgotten memories flooded in; the memory of riding in the back of a police car after being found at the beach; of Danny being swept out to sea as he clung to their dog. That image flashed repeatedly and wouldn't stop. She remembered the undertow — of never feeling anything so powerful — how it gripped her ankles and knocked her down as if she were a twig.

"Miss? Do you know the pilot?" Fran vaguely heard what the police officer was asking her. She could see reporters coming closer, carrying their cameras. Fran told him her name and Cornelia's. She gave the officer all the information he needed as he led her from the scene and into his police car.

On the way to the morgue, Fran tried to think of whom to call. She wanted to talk to one of the girls but knew that CC would be on a train heading back home by now. Nancy would be leaving the Long Beach base to pick up a P-51 Mustang in Dallas and was probably planning to get there via Snafu airlines. Since Fran didn't know how to reach either of them, she called the last person she wanted to tell.

He answered his phone after the first ring.

"General Pitts speaking."

She could tell from his tone that he knew. *One of the pilots must have told him.* There was no point in saying it out loud. There was a long silence on the telephone line before Fran found her voice.

"It's me," she said, sounding hoarse. "Fran."

"Where are you?" he asked.

"I'm in Texas, at the morgue."

"Stay there. I'll make arrangements for a train to get her — and you — out to Nashville, her hometown. We'll bring you your uniform. Nancy will get it. She's right here in my office. I managed to stop the transport plane she was on when I heard the news. We'll both meet you in Nashville. You stay with her on the train. And Fran, try to avoid any press for Pete's sake, although I'm sure they'll get wind of this. If anyone asks you about it, don't tell them anything."

There was a pause. Then she heard a familiar female voice.

"Fran, it's Nancy. Are you okay?"

Fran closed her eyes and tried to know what she was feeling, but she was having difficulty remembering to breathe. She was in a state of shock, her mind's safety blanket protecting her now from the pain that would be coming. The payment due for the trauma endured. The shock would keep her safe, for now. But she knew it was taking a raincheck.

"Nancy, it was..."

There was a long pause. Fran took a deep breath.

"I found her. I think she died on impact. She was knocked unconscious...she didn't even try to open the hatch."

"We'll need to notify her next of kin as well," she heard General Pitts say. "Cornelia's from a very prominent family, as you know, meaning there's going to be a huge turnout for the funeral service. Dear God, it'll be bigger than a national holiday for that town."

Fran stayed at the morgue and tried to sleep on a bench in the waiting area, but her mind wouldn't let her. Instead, flashbacks of both the crashed plane and the sneaker wave replayed over and over until she thought she would go mad.

She couldn't believe that dear, sweet Cornelia was gone. Her friend, her roommate, her fellow pilot. Fran felt light-headed and exhausted from holding in her emotions. She missed Seamus. She missed her mother. But most of all, Fran missed Danny. And the crushing loss of Cornelia was on top of that pain. The pain buried inside of her heart surged out like a sneaker wave, drowning her in the agony of loss.

CHAPTER 33

Fran left early the following morning to catch the first train to Memphis. There, she would disembark to board another train that would take her to Nashville. When she boarded the train heading to Memphis, Fran was still wearing her flight suit. It was covered in dust from the desert, but it was all she had with her. As the train pulled away from the station, it reminded her of the day she left Seamus and her father.

Without warning, tragedy strikes and snatches the precious ones away. And now Cornelia is gone. Forever. I can't believe I will never see her again.

Fran stared out the window and watched the cattle grazing in the fields.

Just another day for them. Same as yesterday. Like last week, except Cornelia was still alive. That's what's different about today. Fran's head and heart hurt.

When she arrived in Memphis, Fran asked the conductor if the train to Nashville was due soon.

"Yes, sir," he said to her. "It will be here in an hour." With her short haircut, she was often mistaken for a boy.

Another train rolled into the station while Fran waited. As she turned to watch the passengers board, a man resembling her Uncle Conrad caught her eye. He was assisting a well-dressed woman in front of him to board. She was wearing white gloves and a feathered hat. As she turned to hand her ticket to the train conductor, Fran saw something familiar about the gracefulness of that motion. It stirred a hazy memory, but one she couldn't place at that moment.

The train to Nashville arrived and began boarding. Fran walked over to it and waited in line with the rest of the passengers.

Then she remembered.

"Mother," she whispered. She left the line and ran towards the other train, feeling the blood pounding in her ears. Fran scanned every passenger's face until she found her. Her mother looked up then; so much was inexplicably communicated in their eye contact.

They continued to stare at one other as Fran's train to Nashville began rolling away from the station.

A gust of wind swept through the area, carrying a lone dragonfly that flew across Fran's view. She turned her gaze to follow its flight path and saw her train leaving the station. She started running to catch up, but the train was picking up speed. Too tired to continue, she stopped.

"Fine, Universe," Fran said. "You win. I quit."

In that instant, the train slowed to a halt. A tall officer stepped out of the back and reached down to help her climb aboard. Fran breathed a huge sigh of relief.

PART III

"We need more gentleness and sympathy and
compassion in our common human life."

—Ralph Waldo Trine

CHAPTER 34

Once they were both inside the train, Fran clung to the officer who had helped her. Then she broke down and started sobbing uncontrollably.

"Hey, you made it," he said. "It's going to be okay now, buddy. I mean, uh, oh my. I thought you were a...would you like to sit down?"

The young officer helped Fran over to the nearest open seats and sat down beside her.

"I'm so sorry," he said. "It's my fault. I can't see anything without my glasses. I didn't know you were a girl." He put on a pair of horn-rimmed glasses that he had taken from a pocket in his uniform.

He remained quiet while Fran continued to cry. Exhausted, she leaned against his shoulder. Something about him felt familiar to her. Fran closed her eyes, and shortly after that, fell asleep. When she woke, his stare startled her; his glasses magnified his soft brown eyes. He smiled at her and raised one eyebrow. Fran found the gesture disarming.

"You're that famous female pilot who was in the newspaper, aren't you?" he asked as he glanced down at her hands. "You were with that movie star...uh, what's his name. Your ring. It's the one you had on in the photo."

"Yep, that was me," she said, looking down at her hands.

"It was my mother's ring — her father gave it to her," Fran said. "He was an orphan. He named my mother after a lady who ran the orphanages in New Orleans. She was known as 'the mother of orphans.' Her family died from some terrible disease when she was only nine years old. Then she got married, but her husband died and then their only daughter died." Fran sighed. "My mother named me after her. The lady's only daughter. Frances."

"Frances," he said. "I like that name."

"Yeah...anyway, this lady devoted her entire life to caring for orphans. She was considered a saint. Now that, mister," she said, pointing her finger into his chest, "is fortitude. You tell me, how does a soul recover from that amount of loss? Not only recover but transform into a giving being rather than becoming bitter?"

He thought for a few moments before answering.

"I believe it's simply a matter of selflessness," he said, "to sacrifice your life for others, that is. Or perhaps it's an expression of a higher level of what we call love." He smiled. "I don't know the answer, but it would be wonderful to become such an incredible person."

At first, she considered him deranged, or else to have led a very sheltered life. But as corny as what he had said sounded, he seemed genuine to Fran. The caring sort.

"Are you close to your mother?" he asked.

"Not exactly. But I have a photo of her." Fran took a picture out of her shirt pocket and showed it to him. It was the one she used to keep in a frame on her nightstand.

"She's beautiful," he said. Fran nodded.

"Look, these are my parents." The officer took out his wallet and opened it. When he did, several tiny bird feathers drifted to the floor. He showed her a photo of his parents in front of a large brick building.

"Is that your high school?" she asked.

"No, it's our house on Lake Geneva. It's where we summer. It's not far from where we live in Chicago."

Fran knew that millions of people must live in that city — that the odds were impossible. But she asked him anyway.

"Are you, are you," she couldn't remember his name. "Joe's Pigeons?"

He threw his head back and laughed good-naturedly. It made Fran smile.

"That's not my actual name. I mostly go by Joe. Sergeant Joe McCormick. I'm on my way to pick up our latest war veteran. She's a real honey of a bird."

Joe explained to Fran how he ended up on the train. He had hoped to hitch a ride in Long Beach with Snafu airlines to get to Chattanooga, so he could pick up Lefty, one of their pigeons. However, General Pitts and Nancy had flown out with the last transport plane, leaving the sergeant to find another means of transportation.

Typically, an injured bird could travel with its pigeoneer to the Long Beach aviary. However, since Lefty's pigeoneer was in critical condition at the hospital, the chief pigeoneer had asked Joe to pick up the bird and bring him back to Long Beach personally.

"I'm a pigeoneer," he said proudly. "I train pigeons to deliver messages for the army. I taught some birds to fly at night and in fog.

That's why we have an aviary at the Long Beach army base, where there's a big body of water and lots of fog."

"Tell me about it," she said. "I feel like I've spent most of my life waiting for the fog to burn off so I can fly. It's the same in Oregon. That's where I'm from."

"I've heard Oregon's a beautiful place. I'd love to see it someday."

"I wish I could go there right now and show you the ocean." Fran sighed. "It's been a rough few days." *Oh, why did I tell him that? Stop talking.*

"What happened?"

"An accident. She was my friend, one of my fellow pilots. I'm on my way to her hometown for the funeral. I have orders to travel with her to make sure she gets there."

"Frances, I'm so very sorry."

His caring tone forced her to look away quickly and hold her breath so she wouldn't start crying again.

"Why don't you tell me more about pigeon training?" she asked. "I hear you're a bit of a legend."

"Me?" he said. "Nah, my commanding officer, Colonel Poutré, now he's the legend. He taught me the secret to training the birds."

"There's a secret?" she asked.

"All right, all right. I'll tell you the secret, but first let me tell you about this one bird."

It relieved Fran to have something to take her mind off seeing General Pitts, who would probably send her home right after the funeral. And she couldn't bear to think about seeing Cornelia's family, who would have that loss of a beloved look in their eyes. And she had just seen her mother. Fran needed to process that as well. But not now.

The sergeant told her the story of Jungle Jim, a four-month-old black-and-white checkered pigeon he had trained. A group of soldiers had jumped out of a plane with Jungle Jim and landed behind enemy lines. Although they knew the enemy's location and position, they had lost their radio operator during the jump. Their only option was to write the information on a note and put it on the young bird. Jungle Jim flew 200 miles at night, above 12,000-foot mountain ranges, and delivered their message.

"Well then, what's the secret?" Fran asked, leaning close to him. "Why do they do it? You know, risk their lives. How do you train them to go against their instincts?"

"The colonel says the secret is to use love and kindness when training them. They used to starve the birds and use food as a motivator to return home, but we found that kindness works even better. Although, you have to be sincere. They can sense your intention, and they trust you. I have to hand it to him; the results from training these birds have been astounding. I know, it's hard to believe, but there's something to it, let me tell you."

"Oh, I believe it. I trained a pigeon to deliver messages. I found him in the forest while ravens were attacking him. He just climbed on my finger."

"Ah, sounds like a conspiracy. It's quite common behavior for ravens."

"I brought him home with me and took care of him until his injuries healed. I take him with me when I fly alone."

Joe looked over his glasses and smiled at Fran, then leaned in closer.

"We believe unconditional love exists," he continued in a low voice. "Well, why not in a bird? They're intelligent creatures. Do you know they can recognize faces? They also recognize kindheartedness, and they want to reward you for it. They risk their lives to deliver messages. Somehow, the birds know the significance."

"Do you love them?" she asked. "The birds?"

Joe grinned and nodded.

His crooked smile made Fran's heart flutter.

"I believe they sense when there is love behind our actions," he replied.

Fran had never heard anyone speak so candidly about love or about creatures. *The birds can sense he's a caring person.*

"Hunters shot Lefty during a pigeon shoot event. A boy who was at the show brought him to me. Hunters have no use for the wounded ones. I repaired his wing as best I could, and after he healed, I trained him for overseas duty. He flew two hundred and thirty miles over the English Channel in four hours, the fastest ever recorded speed. A falcon attacked him during the trip, and he needed twenty-two stitches to fix him up after that. That would be like you getting three thousand stitches. Can you imagine? But despite his injuries, he delivered a message from his fellow airmen after their plane crashed. That's how they were rescued. I'm going to Chattanooga right now to get him and bring him back to Long Beach."

The train slowed down as they approached the Nashville station. Joe stood up. Fran noticed his height then — he was over six feet tall and moved with the poise of someone much older.

"Frances," Joe said, looking out the window, "never underestimate the power of a kind deed."

CHAPTER 35

When the train arrived in Nashville, Fran could see General Pitts and Nancy waiting in a car parked behind the station. She could also see reporters with cameras ready.

Fran and Joe stared out at the row of journalists waiting on the platform. He placed his hand gently on her shoulder.

"Great," she said. "The press is here. The general will send me home for sure if I get my photo in the paper again."

"You stay here on the train," Joe said, "and don't get out until I give you the signal."

Before leaving, he turned and held out his hand. Fran placed her hand in his. His touch was gentle yet firm.

"It was a pleasure meeting the famous female ferry pilot," he said with a twinkle in his eye.

Fran tried not to laugh. *If the reporters see that, they'll make it look like I'm having the time of my life while I'm on my way to Cornelia's funeral.*

"I, too, am grateful to finally meet the legendary pigeoneer, Sergeant Joe McCormick."

Before letting go of her hand, Fran noticed he had held onto it for a moment longer than necessary — maybe a sixteenth of a second. She liked that.

From the window of the train, Fran watched Joe speak to the conductor. As they unloaded the casket, the sergeant stood at attention while reporters snapped photos. General Pitts walked over and stood at attention beside him.

After the hearse left, Joe waved as a signal for Fran to get off the train. She jumped down and tried to run through the line of reporters. As she did, one grabbed her by her parachute strap.

"Say, pal, you seen a girl pilot around here?"

It was Charles.

Before he could recognize her, she shook her head, and he let her go. She turned and continued running towards Nancy. When she got to her, they quickly jumped into the back seat of the rental car.

They watched the reporters without speaking. It started raining. The drops pattering on the roof of the car broke the silence.

"Cornelia had more experience flying those planes than any other ferry pilot," Nancy said. "They were flying in formation, weren't they?"

After a long pause, Fran nodded.

Nancy sighed deeply.

General Pitts came over to the car and climbed into the driver's seat. He nodded to Joe. The sergeant saluted him before re-boarding the train.

"Nice kid," the general commented.

He turned around to look at Fran. Then, without saying a word, he turned back around and started the car.

"I have your dress uniform," Nancy said. "It would be nice if you would speak at the service. You two were close. She thought the world of you, you know. She was always telling everyone how incredible you were."

Once again, Fran tried not to cry.

Everyone who knew Cornelia's family attended the service, which included just about everyone in Nashville. Her mother and her brothers were there, Fran met them as well. Her father had passed away a few years before Cornelia had become a pilot. She'd once told Fran that he'd forbidden his sons to get in an airplane, that they were too dangerous. It had never crossed his mind to tell his daughter.

Cornelia wouldn't have let him stop her anyway, Fran thought.

As Fran walked up to speak, she passed by Charles. He was standing near General Pitts. The reporter attempted to walk towards her, his camera raised, until the general grabbed him.

"No," he said firmly. "Let her be."

"I can't explain to you why I fly," Fran began, "and so I can't put into words why my best friend Cornelia wanted to. She considered it an honor to use her ability to serve our country. And she lost her life doing that. She was happiest when she was in the sky. That's how I'll remember her. It's how she would've wanted you to remember her, too."

After she finished speaking, she heard the whirring sound from reporters' cameras coming from the back of the crowd. As Fran left with General Pitts and Nancy, she walked by Charles. She could feel his eyes on her, but she refrained from turning to look back at him.

CHAPTER 36

After seeing her mother at the train station, Fran couldn't stop thinking about her. She asked the general for three days of leave before carrying out another ferrying assignment so she could look for her mother. Realizing how short-handed they would be without CC or Cornelia, the general reluctantly agreed. But only on the condition that after her leave ended, Fran would travel to Dallas to ferry the P-51 Mustang Nancy had been scheduled to pick up before the accident.

Fran assumed she could find her mother in New Orleans, her hometown. She had never been there, but her Uncle Conrad and Aunt Elsa had told her she was always welcome.

Fran's grandfather had passed away in his sleep at a young age. He left his three children a small fortune, along with a struggling restaurant that they turned into one of the finest establishments in New Orleans. He had come from a humble beginning. He emigrated to America from Ireland with his parents, but they left him at an orphanage in New Orleans because they were too poor to feed him.

Fran knew Aunt Elsa would love for her to take over the restaurant one day. She hadn't considered it before, but now that her mother was probably living there, she thought it was possible.

During the train ride to New Orleans, she wrote a letter to Seamus, remembering Cornelia's promise to visit him. She didn't want to write about the accident, but he may have read about it in the news. She wanted to let him know that she was okay. Frances also wrote a letter to her mother. She planned to give the letter to her aunt if necessary. After seeing her that day, Fran was no longer angry about her leaving. She thought she understood why. She sensed her mother was sad. Only it wasn't about Fran at all. Her mother seemed to be drowning inside herself. And all Fran wanted now was to save her.

When she arrived in town, the city was alive with the sound of jazz music coming from the bars downtown. The streets were cobblestone, something Fran had never seen in Oregon. Colorful flowers adorned balconies with their vines hanging down into the streets.

She couldn't remember the name of her mother's family restaurant, but she knew it was in the French Quarter. She walked up and down Bourbon Street, looking at restaurant names to see if one jogged her memory. There were more restaurants in New Orleans than she was expecting. She kept catching her shoes on the cobblestone cracks, each time nearly tripping her. The stifling heat of downtown made her sweat profusely. Discouraged but not ready to give up, Fran hailed a cab and climbed in the back seat.

"I'm looking for the fanciest restaurant in town," she said to the driver. "But I can't remember the name."

"Joe & Finch?" the driver asked.

"No, it's a sort of funny name," she said.

"Chubby's?"

"Yes! Yes, that's it!"

The restaurant's name was an inside joke within the Irish family. It was her grandmother's nickname, only she was actually quite thin. The cabbie drove a few blocks down Bourbon Street and dropped Fran off in front of the restaurant's dining entrance. She paid him and stepped out of the cab.

The restaurant was dark and cool inside, a welcome retreat from the oppressive heat. After her eyes adjusted to the dim lighting, Fran could see white linen tablecloths and lit candles set on each of the tables.

"Oh, my goodness. Oh, my goodness. Would you look at what the cat dragged in — why they're letting just about anyone in here these days!"

That Irish lilt. Fran hadn't heard it since her mother left.

"Child!" Aunt Elsa exclaimed. "Let me have a look at you. What happened to your hair?" She rushed over and gave Fran a big hug. "Why, I think I like it!"

"You are nothing but skin and bones, don't the army feed you? Come on now. You sit yourself down right here."

Fran did as she was told.

"I'm going to have someone bring us some dinner."

Her aunt called out to one of the waiters. He was wearing the staff uniform; a black suit with a pressed white shirt.

"Harold, bring us two specials. This is my niece, my sister's daughter. And bring me an Old Fashioned. Wait, bring two. She looks like she needs one."

The waiter nodded. "Yes, madam."

"I saw your picture in the *Times-Picayune*," she said with a smile. "My goodness gracious, I was so proud of you! We have that news clipping over on the wall up in front when you first walk in. I tell everyone that comes in here it's my niece. She's a pilot for the army."

Fran smiled, too. It felt wonderful to know someone in her family was proud of her.

Over dinner, they caught up on what had happened since they last saw one another. They were careful to avoid bringing up the person they both knew Fran was there to see. After they finished dinner, Fran couldn't hold it in any longer. She told her aunt she had seen her mother at the train station.

Her aunt whistled a low whistle and then grew silent.

"I assumed she was coming out here," Fran said and took a sip of her drink.

"Wow," she said, swallowing the liquor. "That's strong."

"I figured as much. So that's why you came out here?"

Fran nodded, her throat still burning from the whiskey.

Aunt Elsa looked around the room before speaking. "She isn't sure where she wants to be, child. Oregon didn't suit her. You need to know, she's not as strong as you are, she's well...kind of an interesting one. That's all I'm going to say about it."

"I would like to see her. I want to tell her something."

"It's late. Why don't you spend the night here? We live upstairs over the restaurant and have plenty of spare rooms. I'll have one made up for you."

CHAPTER 37

Uncle Conrad joined the two of them the next morning for breakfast on the patio. Wanting to know more about the power of thought, Fran asked her uncle if simply imagining an outcome could manifest it into reality.

"Yes, indeed — it's a powerful thing," he told her. "Imagination, that is. Only don't spend your life focusing on the future. You need to live in the moment. Let yourself be surprised when it happens. Sometimes you'll receive something even better than what you thought of, but you have to keep a positive outlook while you're waiting."

"Now take your mother, for example," her uncle continued, "she's not able to have a positive outlook. Some just can't."

"Your mother, love," Aunt Elsa said, "is... not in her right mind."

"Never has been," Uncle Conrad interjected.

"Hush!" Aunt Elsa slapped his arm. "Never mind."

"Frances is an adult. It's time she knows the truth."

Aunt Elsa paused thoughtfully before she spoke.

"Your mother tends to become very depressed. She tried to commit suicide when she was sixteen. After that, she stayed in an institution for a month until they released her — said she was 'cured.' Only she wasn't any different after that. Not really."

"After your brother's accident," Uncle Conrad said, "she was planning to admit herself to the nuthouse out in Oregon, voluntarily."

"That's not what they call it!" Aunt Elsa said.

"The insane asylum, excuse me."

"Fran, he's talking about the state institution. Your father insisted she not go. He didn't think it was safe for her."

"That's a bunch of hogwash," Uncle Conrad said. "He didn't want anyone to find out, that's all. It's a sad world we live in when we all have to be so ashamed about something tragic like this."

"Your mother is afraid, Fran," Aunt Elsa said. "So afraid. She isn't like you, you know. So fearless. She thought you knew. She said you were intuitive and that you knew."

Aunt Elsa was quiet for a moment as she struggled with what she was about to say.

"After what happened to Danny, your mother left Oregon and came here. She was afraid she would walk into the ocean and drown herself — or something worse. Your mother didn't want to, well, do anything to hurt you kids or your father."

"I was bringing her back here when you saw us," Uncle Conrad said. "They won't keep folks too long in those places. They can't help people like her, anyway."

"She has insight," Aunt Elsa said. "Your mother is aware enough to know she has something wrong with her. That's something very rare, I will say that much. Although she's still unable to control her actions."

"Anyway," Fran's uncle said, "now she's back in the institution that she went to when she was sixteen. They'll make her leave in a few months, and she'll most likely come back here to stay with us, I imagine."

"Can I see her?" Fran asked.

Her aunt and uncle looked at each other.

"She would never want you to know she was there," Aunt Elsa said. "She'd die of shame."

Fran hadn't expected that answer. The words dealt a harsh blow. Aunt Elsa reached over and hugged her close as tears streamed down her face. Fran could feel the compassion in her aunt's embrace. She yearned for a loving touch. It was so rare that she experienced it.

"I need to leave here today," Fran sobbed. "I have to be on a train to Dallas."

"Well then," her uncle said, "why don't we drive you there, dear."

On the way to the train station, Fran caught a glimpse of a statue.

"Is that Margaret," she asked, "the lady who ran the orphanages?"

"Yes, it is," her aunt said. "Would you like to see?"

Fran nodded. Uncle Conrad pulled over, and they climbed out of the car to have a closer look.

"Pop sure loved her," he said as they admired the monument in honor of Margaret Haughery. "When his parents left him at the orphanage, he was nothing but skin and bones. He would've starved to death if it weren't for her. She took him in and treated him just the same as if he was her own son. She's a veritable saint that one, grandest lady ever lived. If we could all be half as kind to one another as she was."

At the train station, Fran handed her aunt a sealed envelope with her mother's letter inside.

"Aunt Elsa, can you please give this to her for me?"

Fran's aunt looked worried as she took the letter.

"It's all good, I promise," Fran reassured her.

"You're very young to believe," Uncle Conrad said. "Most understand the power of thought much later in life, but some never do."

As Fran boarded the train to Dallas, he offered her some last words of advice. "Just imagine your goal as too big to measure, and you will receive more than you could ever possibly dream of."

CHAPTER 38

When Fran ferried the P-51 plane from Dallas to Seattle, it was the first time she flew alone without Easter. She missed the companionship he brought her and was looking forward to returning to the base to see him.

When Fran arrived at the women's barracks, she could hear Easter's familiar chirping. As she went over to the window sill where he was perched, she noticed someone had left a letter on her bunk. Hoping it was from Seamus, she opened it and read the note inside.

Dear Frances,

I wanted to write to you and offer my sincerest condolences for the loss of your friend. I think of you often and wonder how you are getting along. Please let me know if there is anything I can do for you.

Yours Truly,

Joe

Sergeant J. McCormick, Pigeoneer

U.S. Army Signal Corps, Pigeon Service

Fran put his note in her front pocket, along with her mother's photo. She didn't know why, but just the thought of him made her heart feel lighter. Over the past few days, her mind often wandered to the time on the train when they had first met.

But when General Pitts called Fran to meet him in his office, she felt her heart sink. "This is it," she said to Easter. "Guess we'll be heading back to New Orleans."

When she arrived, she was expecting him to tell her they were ending Project Peanut. Or that they no longer needed her.

But she was mistaken.

"As you know," he began, "we only asked that you stay in the ferrying program for three months. And your three-month stint ends soon."

Fran nodded as she held her breath.

The general stared at her intently, then smiled. "Truth is, Finkel, you're my best pilot. I'll do whatever it takes to keep you on for as long as I can."

She sighed with relief. "I'd like that very much."

"How do you feel about flying the B-25 Mitchell bombers?" he asked.

Fran's eyes flew open wide.

The first time they scheduled her to ferry a B-25, she had given up the assignment to another pilot so she could transport the general and Nancy to Washington. Since then, that same pilot had become the primary ferry pilot for the B-25s.

"That would be incredible," she said.

"Good. They asked me to oversee the transferring of the used-up ones to a boneyard near our base, and I need an extraordinary pilot for the job. Make no mistake, I consider all my pilots to be excellent pilots, or else I wouldn't have them flying. But I need someone who is mechanical as well."

The general explained how the planes would be in rough shape since student pilots had abused them. In addition, some ships had flown overseas where the enemy had shot them, and they would no longer meet the reliability standard required for training or fighting overseas.

"Why do the planes need to go to a boneyard?" she asked.

"Easier for accounting to see what's salvageable. Maybe they'll use some for parts and scrap the remains. If you're interested, I sure can use you. It's a little more dangerous, I — "

"I'll do it," she said before he could finish.

The B-25s were currently being used as combat trainers at army bases all over the country. Colonel James Doolittle flew one of sixteen over to Japan for a surprise attack. It made headlines in all the newspapers. Fran knew her father must have just burst with pride over it. *His hero.* He would probably pin the news clipping on the wall in the hangar's office. The thought of it made her smile.

Before Fran would pick up her first B-25, the general insisted she complete a refresher course on emergency procedures. The program reviewed issues a pilot may face, including dealing with a fire or what to do if an engine quits. Fran also practiced jumping out of a bomber plane while wearing a parachute.

After completing her training, Fran picked up her first B-25 for what would be its very last flight. The military had used the plane for advanced combat training at the Columbia Army Airbase in South Carolina. After checking the plane out with the army mechanics, she started the ship. Fran taxied down the runway, and the B-25 lifted into the sky.

Finally, this was her dream come true. She couldn't help smiling as she turned out to fly the bomber to its final destination, Cal-Aero Field, located 90 miles from the Long Beach base. This would be where most of the planes would eventually enter retirement.

Overall, the planes were still exceptionally reliable. They could endure an incredible amount of abuse, and the rare engine failure would still allow a well-trained pilot to remain in flight or land safely.

During flight training, Fran had learned about the aerodynamics of flying a plane with two engines. If one engine quits, it was possible to fly with only one working engine, as long as the pilot turned the plane towards the side with the working engine. However, a pilot should never turn the aircraft to the side with the dead engine because the aerodynamics of flight would make it impossible to straighten out of the turn to land.

Fran spent the next few months flying worn-out bomber planes to the boneyard, sometimes ferrying them from the other side of the country. Delivering the ships to their last resting place with Easter gave Fran a sense of purpose. They were magnificent beasts that had given their all, these veterans of war on their last flight. She felt it was an honor to serve them.

Fran ferried her first few B-25s without experiencing any incidents. However, during her fifth assignment one of the aircraft's engines failed as she flew over Arizona's scorching desert. Fran managed to turn the plane around and fly it straight to the nearest airport, where she landed on the runway as smoke poured out of the failed engine.

She talked to Easter during those flights, and sometimes she spoke to Cornelia and sometimes Danny. After learning about her mother, Fran thought it was best to stop trying to avoid her feelings. She also realized that flying warplanes wasn't as fulfilling as she was expecting it to be. Instead, she felt lonely and longed to share these moments with someone. In her letter to her mother, Fran wrote about her breakup with John and leaving home to fly for the army. She hoped her mother would be proud of her. Fran also hoped it would make her mother want to return home.

CHAPTER 39

Fran stood outside with the military personnel on a hot June morning, waiting for an army transport plane. She was wearing her wool dress uniform with Easter tucked away inside the breast pocket. Fran's short, boyish haircut had grown out, and the hair against the back of her neck felt damp with sweat. She looked around for shade and picked up her travel duffel bag that had her flight suit, Easter's cage, and her parachute packed inside it. That was when she saw him. He was walking towards her.

It was the first time she had seen Joe since their encounter on the train. She resisted an overpowering impulse to run over and throw her arms around his neck. Her feelings for him felt strangely familiar.

Fran had wanted to go back to the aviary, but whenever she was at the base, she didn't have time. Since Cornelia's death, she had only made it back nights and typically left first thing in the morning to pick up a B-25. It was too sad to stay in her room, alone.

When their eyes met, Fran blushed.

He looked down and smiled that crooked smile of his.

She sighed.

"Well, now," Joe said, "we meet again." Fran picked up an Irish lilt when he spoke. She hadn't noticed it before.

"Hey there," she said, trying to sound nonchalant. She didn't want it to be evident that she had a crush on the sergeant.

A transport plane taxied over to the group, and after shutting it down, the pilot and copilot hopped out. The copilot was Fran's ex-boyfriend.

"Where are you headed?" she asked.

"Wherever you want, Finkel," John said over his shoulder as he walked away. "She's all yours. We're done with her."

"What are you saying, Sorenson? That I need to fly her?"

"Yep, if you want to go someplace, that is."

Once they realized a female was about to be their pilot, half of the officers walked away.

"Oh, come on, you bunch of fraidy-cats!" Fran shouted after them.

"I'm heading north," she told the waiting men. "I can drop any of you off, but I am not going to the East Coast today."

She heard a few of them curse under their breath. Only four remained, including Joe. He looked at her as he cleared his throat.

"Where are you flying today?" he asked.

"Pendleton, Oregon. I'm going to pick up a B-25 and deliver it near our base. I'm hoping to do it in one day and be back here tonight."

General Pitts had let Pendleton's commanding officer know someone was coming for one of his bombers to scrap it. Although Fran wasn't too keen on meeting up with Colonel Von Lekker again, she wasn't about to let the weasel stop her from getting her job done.

"I need to be in New Jersey by Thursday for a secret training program," Joe said. "Trouble is, a train would take too long. So I suppose I'll take a flight to the East Coast tomorrow."

Joe waved goodbye and turned to leave.

"You ever fly in a B-25?" Fran asked, her mind entertaining the possibility of him sitting beside her in the cockpit.

He turned back and shook his head.

"You want to change that?" Fran said. "I could use the company. It gets kind of lonely up there."

She waited for him to answer and thought he was mulling it over — the idea of it.

I know, a girl pilot. I get it.

"Why, of course," he said emphatically. "I'd love to fly with you."

His response took Fran by surprise. Most other men balked at flying with a female pilot.

"Okay, anyone who wants to be somewhere north of here, climb aboard and make it snappy," she said briskly. "I haven't got all day."

Fran turned on her heels and walked over to inspect the plane while the officers boarded the aircraft. She wanted Joe to sit in the cockpit with her but didn't want to ask him in front of the other men, knowing they'd make a big deal of it. After completing her checklist, Fran put on her flight suit and climbed into the pilot's seat. She took Easter from her pocket and placed him in his cage.

After taking off, Fran landed at the Castle Air Force Base and then Mather Army Airfield, dropping off flight instructors at both locations.

When she landed in Pendleton, Fran went into the back of the plane to find Joe. He was the only passenger left. When he saw her, he stood and gestured for her to go before him.

"The pilot is always the last one to leave," she said. "But first, I have something to show you. Come with me."

As Fran walked back to the cockpit, Easter started chirping.

"Hey, wait a minute!" Joe exclaimed. "I know that sound."

They both crouched down as Fran opened Easter's cage. The bird hopped out and climbed up Joe's arm. He softly stroked the bird's feathers.

"I don't believe it," Joe said.

"Do you know if he's a passenger pigeon?" she asked.

"I'm sure he is," he answered, his voice trailing off in amazement. "And he's magnificent."

"He likes you," she said.

He glanced up and grinned at her. Fran felt goosebumps when he did that.

"We'd better go," she told him. "Here, you can carry him for me."

As they disembarked from the transport plane, Joe carried his overnight bag and Easter, now back in his cage. Fran took her flight bag and slung her parachute over her shoulder as they walked towards the guard shack together. The same old guard she ran into last time was on duty.

"I'm here to see the colonel," she told him.

He squinted his eyes at her.

"Is he expecting you?" the guard asked.

"Tell him the pilot's here to pick up a B-25," she said curtly.

The guard looked at Joe and gestured for him to go to the office.

"She's the pilot," Joe said, pointing at Fran.

The guard gave her a dirty look, but this time she wasn't going to tolerate his rudeness. Instead, she gave him an icy stare and didn't break it until he looked away.

"Go on then," he said.

"What was that all about?" Joe asked her as they headed towards the office.

"He doesn't like me. I'm not sure if it's because I'm Jewish or a girl or both."

When Fran and Joe went into Colonel Von Lekker's office, someone else was sitting behind the colonel's desk. He looked familiar, but Fran couldn't recall where she had seen him. He stood up immediately when they entered his office and walked over with his hand outstretched.

"General Pitts told me you were coming," he said to Joe. "Said you're the best pilot in his squadron."

"Sir, I'm not a pilot," Joe said. "I'm a pigeoneer."

"Well, that explains why you're carrying a bird with you."

Fran stood by, amused.

The high-ranking officer raised an eyebrow at her and then put his hand to his mouth.

"I'm Frances Finkel," she said. "I'm the pilot the general was referring to."

She held her hand out graciously, and he shook it. He grinned at her with a twinkle in his eye.

"Well done. Well done. Colonel James Doolittle here, but you can call me Jimmy."

Fran's jaw dropped in amazement.

"*The* James Doolittle?" Fran asked.

He nodded unassumingly.

"You're the commanding officer that led the recent attack on Japan!" Joe exclaimed.

"Don't believe what you read in the papers. Most of the planes crashed, but we all survived. I'm lucky to be alive and still have a job."

Fran just stared at him, dumbfounded.

"Don't you just love flying those big ships?" he said, winking at her.

She nodded enthusiastically, tongue-tied. Her father was right; this man was captivating. She was at a loss for words.

"Thank you for taking care of the retired ones," Doolittle continued, "it's a great service to your country."

"It's nothing compared to what you did," Fran said, finally finding her voice. "I think you're incredible — everyone does. You're a hero."

He waved her comments away.

"Let me find you that paperwork for the B-25 so we can get you on your way."

Together, they went through all the documentation for the ship, and Fran filed the required flight plan. She had completed aircraft paperwork at least a hundred times before but never with someone even more meticulous about it than she.

The colonel nodded at Joe.

"Son, you flying with Miss Finkel in the B-25?" he asked.

"Yes, sir," Joe said.

Doolittle rummaged around behind the desk and pulled up a parachute pack.

"Here then, take my parachute," he said, handing it to Joe. "My plane went down in Mexico. I had to repair it before I could fly out, but it was stuck in a deep canyon. So I sent a note on a pigeon, asking for the tools I needed."

"And you got out?" Fran asked.

"Of course!" Doolittle said. "I'm here, aren't I?" He grinned. "A pilot flew over and dropped what I asked for."

"Unbelievable," she said.

Joe eyed his gift questioningly.

"That's my lucky parachute, McCormick. It saved my life three times."

"I wish I could have been there on your squad," Fran blurted out, "flying one of the B-25s."

"The country will come around to allowing women pilots in the army one day, so don't give up that hope."

Fran nodded to him as they were leaving.

"Safe travels, my friends," Colonel Doolittle said.

A red-haired, freckled-faced officer sat in a jeep in front of the building, waiting to drive Fran and Joe out to the bomber plane.

"You the pilot for the B-25?" he asked Joe.

"No." He nodded to Fran. "She is."

She glared at freckle-face.

Do not say a word.

He didn't.

They climbed into the jeep, and the officer headed down a road lined with various types of warplanes. It was an open jeep and too loud to speak. Joe remained deep in thought as he stared at Easter in his cage.

The jeep stopped at the B-25 assigned to Fran. It was in deplorable condition. She noticed the tires were flat and assumed it had been sitting there for a while.

The weasel must've found the worst plane he could scrape up for my first assignment here.

Joe looked at her, bewildered.

"Are we seriously going to fly in that piece of junk?" he asked. "Is that why I need a parachute?"

"We'll need air in those tires," Fran told the driver as she jumped out of the jeep to inspect the plane.

"Yes, ma'am," the officer said. She went through the seventy-five items on the checklist, noting down several issues that caused the plane to fail her inspection. Then, she handed the list to the officer.

"I'll need those items taken care of before I can fly it," she told him. "They're minor. The mechanics should be able to get through that list in less than an hour. Can you drive us to the airport diner and pick us up when the plane's ready?"

"Of course."

The officer drove them to the diner and dropped them off at the front door. Joe had to duck his head to enter the doorway. They chose a booth and sat across from one another. A short, chubby waitress came over to take their order.

"All right, kids," she said. "What can I get you?"

Fran ordered a grilled cheese sandwich and a grape soda.

"And for you, darling?" she said to Joe.

"Yes, ma'am. I'll have the same, please."

The server took their menus.

"Thank you very much," she said, winking at Joe.

After the waitress left, Joe looked deep in thought.

"I can't believe we just met Jimmy Doolittle in person," Fran said. "AND he gave you his parachute. I wish I could tell..." her voice trailed off as she thought of her father. She suddenly realized she missed him.

"Tell me, Frances," Joe said. "What's your boyfriend do? Is he a pilot, too?"

Fran paused for a moment before answering him. *He's feeling out my situation. So sly.*

"I don't have a boyfriend. Well, I did. He's that copilot who flew in this morning. He's kind of a jerk."

"Well, he's definitely a jerk if he let you slip away."

"It's okay, that's ancient history. I was young and didn't know what love was then."

"Here you go," the waitress said, placing the meals down on their table. "Good golly, if you two aren't the cutest couple I've ever laid eyes on."

Joe took off his glasses and polished them.

"She thinks we're a couple," Joe whispered.

Fran loved that she did.

"Yeah, right," he chuckled. "Guy like me with a looker like you, ha, now that's a hoot." Joe put down his glasses. "I like you, Frances. You're not like the other girls, not always worrying about your hair and makeup or how you look."

Is that supposed to be a compliment? Now, what should I say? Ask if he has a girlfriend? That would be too obvious. No need to get all sappy here. No need to let him see that I've fallen for him. Instead, she thought it safer to let him believe she didn't care for him one bit. *Must protect the heart.* Fran wondered if he'd ever kissed a girl. *Do not ask that.*

"Do you believe in love at first sight?" she asked.

Smooth. Way to go.

"Yes," Joe said. He looked away.

"But I believe in lots of things," he stammered nervously, "that most people don't."

He picked up his sandwich and took a bite.

"Like what?" she asked.

He looked away as he chewed.

"I believe in thoughts, like to get what you want."

Fran stared at him as she listened intently to what he was saying.

"I know, it's strange. It's just what I believe is all."

"You mean you believe in the laws of attraction and how you can have what you want by thinking about it?"

"Yes! That's right. Why, I've never actually met anyone who has even heard of it."

Fran was about to tell him how she'd fallen in love — love at first sight — when she saw the officer who drove them in the jeep waving to her from the parking lot.

"We'd better get going," she sighed.

Joe paid for their meal, and they left the diner to climb back into the jeep.

The mechanics had inflated the plane's tires and fixed the issues Fran had found. However, she went through every item on the checklist again, making sure everything still passed her inspection.

"Poor old girl, they really beat you up, didn't they?" Fran said, running her hand along one of the bullet-ridden sections. "That's all done with. I'm going to take you home. This is going to be your final flight."

She started to put her parachute on over her flight suit. Joe stood by, amused.

"Watch me," she said. "I'm going to help you put on your parachute once I have mine on."

She already had her chute on her back when she brought two straps up under her legs and buckled them. Then she buckled the remaining straps across her chest.

"See?" she said. "Easy, right?"

He looked oddly at his parachute and held it disdainfully away as if it was a dead fish.

She laughed as he slung the chute up onto his back.

"These straps," she said, pointing to her lower straps, "they go under your legs like this, see?"

He stepped into the straps and tried pulling them up between his legs. Fran watched and shook her head.

"I'm not helping you with that part," she told him. "That's for you to figure out."

Once Joe managed to pull the lower straps up between his legs, Fran helped him lock the clasp at his beltline and then snapped his chute's chest buckle, gently tugging it to make sure it was snug.

"Good job, sergeant," she said, holding on to his straps. Fran was tempted to pull him closer but pushed him away playfully instead.

She had a plane to deliver.

They both climbed the ladder that dropped from the plane's trapdoor. Fran showed Joe where the gunner would sit in the plane's nose before they went to the cockpit. They placed their travel bags on the floor behind the two pilot seats. Joe placed Easter's cage down while Fran prepared for takeoff.

"You need to wear these," she said, handing him one of the pilot headsets hanging in the cockpit. "Unless you want to go deaf from the noise."

They each donned their headsets. Joe's knee was touching lightly against Fran's leg. She didn't move away.

"Can you hear me?" she said into her mouthpiece.

"No," he said back into his as he shook his head.

She chuckled at his joke and then looked around the area.

"Clear!" Fran yelled out the window. She pressed the ignition switch and held it. The engines coughed a bit as the propellers on each side began turning. The mechanics stood by at a safe distance with a fire extinguisher handy.

"Hey, it started!" she kidded.

Joe laughed nervously. "What have I gotten myself into?"

Fran completed the startup procedure before releasing the brakes.

As she taxied the soon-to-be-retired bomber plane towards the runway, she contacted air traffic control for permission to take off.

"Say souls on board," the control tower asked her.

Joe grinned and held up three fingers.

"Three souls," she answered.

After being cleared for takeoff, Fran taxied past the other parked planes and out onto the airstrip. She pushed the throttle forward, and when they reached over 100 miles an hour, the plane lifted off the runway. Fran turned to a westerly heading as they left the airfield behind them. Once they had climbed to cruising altitude, she spoke first.

"We should arrive in about five hours. The scrapyard is close to Long Beach. An officer will drive us back to our base after we deliver the plane."

"I have to be honest," Joe said, "I'm impressed. I've never flown up in the cockpit with the pilot before. Say, where did you learn to fly?"

"My father has a maintenance shop in Oregon, where I grew up. I've been flying planes or fixing them for as long as I can remember."

"I've never been to Oregon, but someone once told me it's nice there."

"You should go then," Fran said. She glanced over at him.

"Definitely."

They were silent for a moment.

"You must also come to Chicago then. I can give you a tour of the city."

"I'd like that," she said.

"I can show you the zoo. I worked at the aviary while I was in veterinarian school. You know your bird here is uh, rather special."

"He's a beauty, isn't he?" she said. "I trained him to deliver messages to my father when I'm away from home. I named him Easter because I found him on Easter."

"Frances," Joe said. "You know, Easter is no ordinary pigeon."

He paused.

"Easter is a passenger pigeon," he continued, "and the passenger pigeon population was, well, it's hard for us to comprehend. Their flocks were enormous. My grandfather told me he saw one of their nesting areas — it covered eight hundred square miles. He figured there were over one hundred million birds there."

"Million?" she said.

"That's right. Million. I've heard there used to be bigger flocks of more than a billion. They would blot out the sky for days when they migrated. It was like nothing we've ever seen. And not something we ever will, I'm afraid."

Joe paused again.

"You see, there's only one known passenger pigeon still alive. She lives at the zoo. Her name is Martha. I used to believe that once she died, they'd become extinct."

He stopped and looked behind him at Easter.

"But maybe I was wrong."

"I can fly over the area where I found him, so you can see it," Fran said. "It's on our way. Those peaks over on our left are the Three Sisters. That means we're near Bend, Oregon."

Suddenly, Fran heard a disturbing noise. She listened carefully. She thought the left engine had made a grinding sound. It was a noise she had heard only once, right before she'd lost an engine. It made her uneasy. She started to descend, just in case. Fran didn't mention it to Joe, but she continued listening.

She thought she saw the lighting on the cockpit's panel flicker for a second but wasn't sure. Fran knew she had seen an emergency kit somewhere inside the plane. *Where was it?*

The panel flickered again. Fran didn't know if she could land safely if she lost the panel lighting. It wasn't dark, not yet. But the sun was setting, and they were heading over the Cascade Range now. Fran turned the plane to a southeast heading to avoid the mountains. She knew experienced pilots avoided flying near mountains; the treacherous mountain waves could suck planes down into them at incredible speeds. She'd heard the stories of pilots who had flown too close and never recovered their altitude.

"Joe, do you see where it says on that handle to open in case of emergency?" she nodded toward the right side of the plane. "If you push it to the left, it unlocks the trapdoor on the floor. Do you remember where we climbed in?"

"Yes, I do," the sergeant said.

"And do you see that cord on your parachute there in front? After you jump out, you need to wait ten seconds before you pull it. So count to ten first, okay?"

"Jump?" he said, "Out?"

She glanced over at Joe. He looked pale and was breathing fast.

She remembered what her father always said. "Pride kills a lot of pilots," he had told her, "lots more times than engine trouble. A good plane is forgiving of some error, but you need to know when it's time to call it."

This is a good plane. It's a B-25, it can handle some problems. I can even lose an engine and land safely. We're three hours away, just three more hours. Come on, Old Girl.

She could smell something burning. Smoke began drifting into the cockpit.

"Pull that emergency latch now," Fran commanded. "Then take Easter and follow me."

Joe pulled the latch, then watched her flip the fuel emergency shut-off valves.

Fran removed Joe's headset and then her own. He grabbed Easter's cage and his duffel bag, and she held on to his arm. She crept down to the bottom of the plane as Joe followed close behind her. Fran saw the emergency kit hanging on the inside wall. She grabbed it and stuffed it into her flight suit.

Since she had cut the fuel to the engines, Fran knew the plane would lose its lift soon. She prayed it didn't explode before they had time to jump as they knelt over the trapdoor.

"I'm going to push open this door!" Fran shouted over the engine noise. "And then you're going to jump out!"

"What? Wait a minute!" Joe shouted. "How many times have you done this?!"

"I've done lots of practice jumps! Don't worry! It's a piece of cake!" She opened the hatch, and the rush of air pushed them back.

"The slipstream will pull you away from the plane — don't be afraid of it!" Fran shouted.

Joe gritted his teeth as he looked out of the hatch. He tucked Easter's cage under his arm and took a deep breath.

Fran could see he wasn't able to do it. He was shaking. She recalled their conversation on the train. *What was it he had said about motivating a being to do something completely against their instinct? Something dangerous? Life-threatening?*

They had little time. She grabbed Joe by the side straps of his parachute and pulled him close to her.

"Listen to me! I'm not leaving this plane until you jump!"

Joe took one last deep breath, looked into her eyes, then leaned in and kissed her as if it were goodbye before jumping to his fate.

Fran could see the flames licking along the insides of the plane. She counted to three before going after him. After jumping out, the slipstream blew her clear of the ship. Moments later, it exploded. Fran plunged towards earth as burning plane parts dropped around her.

"Please, please, let his chute open," she prayed as she watched Joe below her. "I'll never not believe again, I swear. Eight Mississippi, seven

Mississippi, six Mississippi, five Mississippi, four, please, please, please," she prayed as she counted. "I'll do anything, I swear."

Fran knew that only about one in a thousand parachutes failed to open. Still, all she wanted in the world was for Joe's chute to work. That was when Fran experienced an epiphany. She understood what made her brother Danny, and Joe's pigeons, selflessly rush into harm's way. Because without hesitation, she would risk her life for Joe.

Fran saw a burst of white silk when his parachute opened.

"Thank you!" she cried out.

She reached for her ripcord and pulled, but nothing happened.

Her parachute didn't open.

Fran tried not to panic. She knew her only chance to survive would be if she could grab Joe on her way down. She could hear Danny's voice in her head saying, "Come on, Frankie, you can do it!"

Fran reached out towards Joe and caught one of the cords of his parachute. He dropped his duffel bag and reached out to hold on to her with his free hand, the other still tightly clinging to Easter's cage.

Dusk fell upon the three souls as they floated in the twilight sky.

Fran looked at Joe clutching Easter's cage and realized she never would have met him if she hadn't found that bird. She wondered if Doolittle would have given Joe his parachute if a pigeon hadn't once helped him.

What sleight of hand is behind all of this?

As they drifted into the Oregon wilderness, Fran realized something quite grand must be looking out for her.

CHAPTER 40

As the wind carried them towards the forest floor below, Joe's parachute caught in one of the tall cedars. He pulled a knife from his back pocket and started cutting the parachute cords caught in the tree. Fran grabbed a large branch for balance.

"Are you okay?" he asked her.

"Be careful, Joe! Don't cut all the cords."

She took a rope out of her duffel bag and threw the bag so it would clear the trees.

"We're lucky it's not dark yet," she said. "We can see how high we are in this tree."

She tied the rope to the large branch she had been holding onto and began to slide down the tree. She was about ten feet from the ground when the branch snapped.

When Fran fell, Joe was climbing down from the tree by grabbing branches with his free hand.

"Frances!" Joe shouted.

He dropped to the ground near her.

"Are you okay?" he asked. "Are you hurt?"

Fran moaned in pain. She rolled down her stocking to look at her injury.

Joe bent down and examined her swollen ankle.

"I don't see any bones," he said. "That's a good thing."

He helped Fran up, but when she tried to put any weight on her ankle, it hurt too much. She sank back down to the ground.

Joe found the emergency kit that Fran had taken from the plane and found a bandage inside. He knelt to wrap it around her ankle as Fran watched. Something about the tenderness in the way he touched her made her want to cry.

"We should get it elevated," he said, standing up. "Here, lean on me. We can walk to that clearing over there, and I'll start a fire. I saw some matches in the emergency kit."

He helped Fran over to a flat spot and propped her foot up on Easter's cage. Then he started gathering dry branches to build a fire.

"Shame," she said. "I really liked that plane. But at least we're all alive."

"Where are we?" Joe asked.

"I'd say we're on the edge of the Oregon-California state border or close to it. We're not due in for about three hours, so they won't come looking for us for a while, and they know if it's dark, they can't find us. It looks like we're going to be here for the night."

Fran looked in the emergency kit. "There's some food in here if you're hungry."

She took out a bag of dried powder and made a face. "We should give Easter something to eat and drink before we free him. I can write out our approximate coordinates so he can let them know where we are."

"Has Easter ever flown at night?" Joe asked. "It's dangerous for him. There'll be birds of prey out there once it's dark. I wouldn't want anything to happen to him."

They both looked down at her pigeon.

"If something happens to Easter," he said, "and he's the second to last passenger pigeon, then..." his voice trailed off. "Well, I can walk to find help instead."

"You could. But you might get lost and starve — or be killed by wolves or a bear."

"How far is it to civilization?" he asked.

"About four hundred miles. At least."

"Do you think the army will find us?"

"It won't be easy. I went off course to avoid the mountains. Besides, I don't think their top priority will be to search for a ferry pilot and a pigeoneer in an about to be scrapped bomber plane."

Although she'd spent many nights outside alone, Fran did not want Joe to leave — and she was trying her hardest to convince him to stay with her.

Joe sighed and took a small cylinder out of his pocket, along with a pen and a thin notebook.

"What's our location?" he asked.

She told him their latitude and longitude as best as she could figure. Joe wrote out their coordinates and noted the time. Fran told him to add the general's phone number before putting the note in the tube. She took Easter out of his cage, and the pigeoneer gently placed the cylinder around the bird's leg.

"Do we have any water?" he asked.

She shook her head.

"Then Easter leaves tomorrow at the earliest," he said. "We may get lucky and find fresh water somewhere around here before we send him. When I train the pigeoneers, I tell them to give their bird water first before they drink any. 'That bird may very well save your life,' I'd say."

Joe added branches to the fire to keep them warm and scare away any predatory animals in the area.

"Easter knows you saved his life," he said. "I have no doubt he would fly out of here and risk being killed for you. I don't know how they know it, but there is some unspeakable way species communicate with other species. We all have this longing to...shine." Joe gazed at her. "Isn't that why you fly?"

The truth was, Fran wasn't sure why she flew. Initially, it was because she loved it. But it had evolved into something else, perhaps a calling to serve.

He sat down beside her, and they watched the fire together. It reminded Fran of her many overnight trips spent at the ocean.

"Tell me about the Oregon Coast," the pigeoneer said, reading her mind. "What do you love about it?"

"Well, it's so untamed — the crashing waves, the wind, the storm-iness. It's almost...restless. And there are giant cedar trees along the coastal cliffs that add to the mystery of it all when it's foggy. It's quite romantic, actually."

Fran told him about her trips to the coast with her brother and how they would watch the sunset over the ocean. Joe looked longingly at her as she spoke.

"I don't have any brothers or sisters," Joe said. "It's just me."

"My twin brother drowned. A rogue wave took his life. I was there when it happened."

"That's terrible."

"Yeah. It was."

"I can only imagine."

"We were both pilots. He believed that flying for the army was in his destiny from the day we were born, September twenty-eighth, 1924. It was the same day two army planes completed the first around-the-world flight. Four planes had taken off from Seattle, but only two planes, named the Chicago and the New Orleans, made it back. Danny and I were delivered at the Portland Hospital, a little south of the landing place."

"What were the names of the other planes, the ones that didn't make it?" Joe asked.

"Boston and Seattle."

"Well, of course, Chicago could beat Boston any day," he said. "Chicago's a much better city than Boston."

Fran laughed, remembering her crush on the Boston reporter. She thought about Joe's goodbye kiss, hoping he would try to make a pass at her like Charles had.

"You know," she said, moving closer to him, "this is quite scandalous. Us, out here alone, unchaperoned. It could ruin my reputation."

"Don't you worry about that. I'm a perfect gentleman. Here, why don't you rest up against my back and sleep a bit?"

He sat with his back to hers, and she leaned on him. Fran felt warm and safe against him, like the time on the train when she had fallen asleep on his shoulder.

"I don't think I ever thanked you for helping me that day we met on the train."

"Ah, don't mention it. You're splendid company. Look at me, getting to spend all this time with such a talented lady. I feel like the luckiest guy on the planet!"

"If you think all that flattery is going to get you another flight in a B-25, you can think again."

"Yes, indeed," Joe chuckled. "I can check that off my to-do list."

They sat in silence, looking up at the sky.

"I've never seen so many stars in my entire life," he said.

"That's because there isn't any civilization for hundreds of miles."

"I have a confession to make," Joe said sheepishly. "I used to keep that newspaper photo of you in my wallet until the day we met."

"Why did you stop after you met me?" Fran asked.

"Strangest thing, that day on the train. I was handing my ticket to the conductor when a breeze came from nowhere and blew the news clipping out of my wallet and right out the window. I looked to see where it went, and I saw you running. I asked the conductor to stop the train, and he did. When I opened the door, there you were."

Fran smiled to herself. She liked that he had kept her photo in his wallet.

"What is your secret training about in New Jersey?" she asked. "If you can't tell me, I understand. I'm just curious."

"Colonel Poutré wants to train pigeons to peck on a button when they see an orange-colored object. This way, search parties can find soldiers floating in the ocean if they're wearing an orange life jacket. We would put the pigeon somewhere inside the plane near a window. They can see ten miles out, even in foggy weather."

Fran drifted off to sleep as she listened to the comforting sound of Joe's voice.

CHAPTER 41

Joe was holding her in his arms when the morning light woke Fran. His fresh scent reminded her of sheets after they'd dried in the summer breeze.

Joe opened his eyes.

"Easter's gone," he said, jumping up.

The bird's cage was empty.

"Maybe he left to find food," Fran said.

"I don't think so. He's on his way home now. Pigeons always fly to their home base — even if it's far away — unless someone's trained them to do otherwise. It's tough to 'unstick' them, that is, have them return to a new location. Easter wasn't trained to do that."

Hoping by now a search and rescue should be well underway, they took the flares out of the emergency kit and waited.

An hour later, they could hear a plane flying overhead. Joe jumped up and lit one of the flares; it glowed as it shot up in the sky. They watched as the plane flew directly over them and then turned back.

"That's Doctor Gato's plane," Fran said. "I don't know why he would be out here. Maybe they released him from the internment camp."

"What's an internment camp?" Joe asked.

"It's where the Japanese are being forced to live since the government thinks they're a threat. It's crazy."

As Fran was telling Joe about how she and Seamus had stumbled upon the camp in Southern Oregon, they saw a figure in the forest walking towards them. Joe helped Fran up and held her protectively.

"Papa?" she cried. "What are you doing here?"

"I was in the neighborhood," her father said dryly. "Thought I'd go for a hike." He noticed Fran standing on one leg. "Are you okay?"

"I hurt my ankle. How did you find us?"

"Easter came to the house," he said.

"He's *still* stuck on his home base in Oregon," Joe said. "Not our base in Long Beach. Like I said, it's hard to unstick them."

"Come on," her father said. "Let's get you two out of here. I had one of my student pilots take us out here. He's waiting for us. Good thing we had Doctor Gato's plane so we could come find you."

"Yes, we're lucky it's not us in the internment camp," Fran said sarcastically.

She leaned on Joe for support as they walked to the plane with her father. Once they were in the aircraft, the student pilot took off with Fran's father beside him in the front seat.

Joe spoke loudly as he leaned forward. "Your daughter is quite the pilot, sir. She saved our lives. If it weren't for her, we'd be dead now."

Fran's father grunted in response.

"How's Seamus?" Fran asked.

"Your brother is good, considering. He's pretty sore at you. He didn't want me to come to find you."

Fran sensed there was something more her father wasn't telling her.

"Papa, what is it?" she asked.

He hesitated. "Easter's hurt. It looks like maybe a hawk, or an eagle, got hold of him. Seamus is with him now."

Fran drew in her breath.

"I was afraid of that," Joe said.

As soon as their plane rolled up at Seal Rock Airport, Seamus stepped out from the hangar.

"Seamus!" Fran cried.

Her brother turned his back when he saw her and stormed away. He had grown so much that Fran hardly recognized him. She tried to jump out of the plane but forgot about her ankle. Joe lifted her out.

"I'm not talking to you!" Seamus shouted back at her. His voice sounded deeper since she'd last heard him speak.

"Seamus!" Fran called out. "I'm sorry! Please try to understand."

He stopped and turned around. "Whatever," he said. "I don't care anymore anyhow. Easter is in rough shape," he said as he continued walking. "I've been staying here with him. I don't know if he's gonna make it."

To keep up with Seamus, Joe picked Fran up and carried her in his arms.

"Where is the bird?" Joe asked, rushing behind him.

"Follow me," Seamus said. He headed inside the hangar towards the office.

Easter was resting on a soft blanket Seamus had taken from Bernice's bed. He had placed a bright light on the bird to keep him warm.

"Yes," Joe said. "This looks like the work of an eagle."

As soon as Fran saw her injured bird, tears began streaming down her cheeks. The thought of losing Easter was too much.

The pigeoneer opened his duffel bag and took out his surgeon's kit. "Do you have any alcohol?" he asked Seamus. "I could also use any first aid items you can find."

Once Seamus brought him the items he had requested, Joe took off his glasses and went to work.

"Oh, Easter," Fran sobbed, "please be all right."

Joe looked over at Seamus and raised one eyebrow at him, cueing him to comfort his sister. Seamus went over and put his arm around her, and she clung to him.

"I can't bear to watch," Fran said. She held her hand over her mouth as tears streamed down her face. "I don't know what I'll do if — "

"How does this guy know how to fix a bird?" Seamus asked, interrupting her.

"He's a pigeoneer for the army," she said, trying to regain her composure. She sighed. "He's second in command to the chief pigeoneer. He trains them to deliver messages for the soldiers."

"Gosh," he said, "you think he can save Easter?"

"Well, we're in luck. Joe's the best there is, so at least we have that going for us."

"Seamus," Joe said, "I believe I could use your help here. Would you be able to assist me?"

"Me?" Seamus replied. He rushed over to Joe and the injured bird. "Heck, yeah. I mean yes, sir!"

Their father entered the hangar.

"Fran, can you come with me?" he asked. He helped her into the truck, and they drove home as Fran continued to weep for Easter. Once they were inside, he made a phone call.

"I have someone here that would like to speak with you," her father said into the phone's receiver. He held the phone out for Fran. She looked at him curiously.

"Hello?" she said into the phone.

"Frances?" she heard General Pitts say into the receiver. "Is that you?"

It was the first time the general called her by her first name.

"Yes, sir...no, I'm okay. I hurt my ankle. Joe's okay, yes. The plane, though...there was a fire." She explained how they had both jumped out before it exploded and crashed into a mountain.

"Glad to know you're both safe," the general said, sounding relieved. "That was one expensive explosion, but it was headed for the scrapyard — better than if it was a new one. I'm sure if my best pilot couldn't save it then nobody could have. Your father called me after your pigeon showed up at your home and said he would go out right away to find you both. Please thank him for me."

After their call ended, she sat down at the table.

Her father was pouring a cup of coffee.

"Tea?" he asked her.

"Coffee, please."

He looked at her, surprised. He tilted his head to the side.

"You're different," he said.

He poured two mugs of coffee and set one down in front of Fran before pulling up a chair. He looked at her for a moment before speaking.

"I'm sure you know how worried I was about you."

Fran looked down at the floor and wrapped her hands around the coffee mug, waiting for the lecture on how guilty she should feel for leaving.

Then her father did something he hadn't done since she was a little girl; he held her face up in his hands.

"It's not right to lose your child. They shouldn't die before you. It's not natural. This war, our country joining in it, means sending so many more children out to die."

Gingerly, she placed her hand on his arm to comfort him.

"You were right," he admitted. "We must try to stop this Jew murderer, this Hitler maniac. I understand now. We must try to save others, no matter the sacrifice."

He looked up at her and smiled. There were tears in his eyes.

"I'm proud of you for leaving. That took courage. I saw your photo in the paper. We have it pinned up in the hangar. I show it to every student that comes in."

Fran smiled at that.

"You should have seen Seamus burst through the front door the day that picture came out," he chuckled. "His arms were full — he bought all the papers, couldn't open the door. I'd never seen him so excited, screaming at the top of his lungs: 'Papa! Papa! It's Fran! She's a pilot for the army! She did it!'"

"Do you think he'll ever forgive me?" she asked.

"He will. Oy vey! He has his mother's Irish temper, but they cool off...eventually."

"I wrote to him all the time. I was hoping he read my letters, but he never wrote back."

"Seamus got your letters. He checked the mail every day — sometimes twice — to see if you wrote. He adores you." Her father stood up. "Who else is he going to worship? Me?"

Her father opened the kitchen drawer where they kept the mail. "Skeeter wrote to you. I wrote to let him know you were ferrying planes for the army. I didn't open his letter. I don't open your mail."

He placed an envelope on the table in front of Fran. "This also came for you."

The letter's postmark was from New Orleans. On the back of the envelope was a wax seal in the shape of a heart.

"By the handwriting on the front, I assume it's from your mother."

CHAPTER 42

Joe managed to mend Easter for the injuries he received on his journey to the Finkel's home. The poor bird needed to wear a leather collar around his neck for support as he healed. Seamus was so inspired by Joe that he decided he wanted to become a veterinarian instead of a reporter.

When Fran found out at the hospital in Newport that her ankle was sprained, she requested six weeks of leave to allow it to heal. She spent that time at home with Easter and Seamus. Her brother was so distracted by caring for Easter that he forgot how mad he was at her for leaving. She was home for now, and that was all that mattered. Seamus made the best of the time he would have with her until she left.

General Pitts told Fran they would abolish Project Peanut at the end of the summer, but there was another effort to train female pilots to ferry planes starting up in Texas. Nancy was already there, and he said he would put in a good word for Fran if she were interested in joining them.

Every morning the first thought Fran had when she woke up and each night as she fell asleep was for her pigeon to recover. Easter healed quickly, and once the bird no longer needed medical attention, Joe hopped on an army transport plane and flew to New Jersey to meet with Colonel Poutré so he could assist with his pigeon training. He called Fran every day — to check on Easter, of course. He said the colonel was intrigued with the idea of breeding the passenger pigeon with homing pigeons, but Joe insisted they let Martha meet Easter first.

Joe's father, a member of the Chicago Zoo's Board of Directors, came up with an idea. Since the zoo invested heavily in protecting and conserving wildlife, he decided to throw a black-tie charity ball to raise awareness of the passenger pigeon's fate. They would then donate the proceeds to a charity that would protect passenger pigeons and other future endangered species. He said he knew many wealthy philanthropists would want to be there.

He was right.

Over three hundred people attended the gala affair. Joe's father arranged for it to be held at the zoo on a summer evening, and he also hired a jazz band to play at the event. Seamus and his father brought Easter to Chicago, flying first class, all expenses paid by Mr. McCormick. Fran flew in with Snafu airlines.

"Hey, handsome, you want to dance?" she asked Seamus when she saw him standing outside of the ballroom with his hands in his pockets, wearing a new suit. He grinned at her and held out his arm. She took it as they strolled over to the dance floor.

"Where's Joe?" Seamus asked as they waltzed across the room.

"He'll be here. He wouldn't miss it for the world."

"I think that's him," Seamus said, nodding towards the entrance. "He just came in."

Fran turned to look in that direction. She hadn't seen Joe since he left Oregon four weeks ago. Looking tan from the summer's sun and sporting a tuxedo and shiny black loafers, the sight of him made Fran's heart race. When she saw him searching the room, she knew he was looking for her. When their eyes finally met, she thought the music had stopped until realizing she had been holding her breath.

"Fran, you okay?" Seamus asked. "You look like you're going to be sick or something."

"I think I'm falling for Joe."

"Does he know?"

"No."

"Well, what are you waiting for? There's a war going on you, know. You may not have forever."

"What would you think if I ran over there and threw my arms around him and kissed him while everyone was watching?"

"Frances Finkel! We are *not* shanty Irish!" Seamus said, mocking their mother.

Fran burst out laughing, and then felt someone gently squeeze her shoulder.

"Something amusing?" Joe whispered in her ear.

"Pardon me, may I cut in?" he asked Seamus, who bowed out graciously as he let the sergeant take his place. Joe placed his hand on the small of Fran's back. It felt familiar, as if he had done so hundreds of times in the past. Or the future.

"How's Easter?" he asked.

"He's doing much better," she said. "You are amazing. I can't believe that he's still alive. You saved his life. I don't know how to thank you."

He smiled and gazed at her as they waltzed across the ballroom floor.

"What will you do with the reward money?" he asked. Now that Easter had been recognized as an official passenger pigeon, Fran would be the reward recipient for finding and caring for him.

"I was thinking of choosing a charity to give it to."

"That's a lot of money."

"Not if it's for a good cause. Besides, it feels good — even just the thought of doing it — being the person who gives. I like it."

"Maybe you're on the path to becoming a saint, like Margaret."

He smiled down at her and gently traced his finger along the back of her ear. Fran wished they were alone.

Joe was an excellent lead, and they danced for over an hour as the band played into the evening.

After the music stopped, Joe's father announced that the newest passenger pigeon was about to meet their resident bird. The crowd wandered out to the aviary to watch Joe bring Easter to Martha's coop. Reporters, eagerly waiting to take photos of the two birds, jumped into action at the sight of Joe. Fran was still avoiding the press, so she watched from a distance. She could see Charles there; scanning over the crowd of guests. When he saw Fran in the back, he winked at her. Fran was feeling so good that before she could stop herself, she smiled back at him.

"Hello, Martha," Joe said.

When he stepped inside her coop, the pigeon recognized him immediately and climbed up his arm.

"I have someone that I want you to meet."

He reverently placed Easter down near Martha. For Joe, this was a moment to cherish.

Reporters clamored around the scene, aiming their cameras as flashbulbs popped. Fran waited until the journalists left before approaching Joe. When she found him, he was standing in front of the aviary building, speaking to a distinguished-looking older gentleman.

"Frances, where have you been?" Joe asked. "There's someone here that I want you to meet."

The stranger turned and faced her.

"Frances," Joe said, "this is my commanding officer, Colonel Poutré, the Army Signal Corps Chief Pigeoneer."

"Such a delight that we finally meet," the colonel said. "I've heard so much about you. I am sorry to say that I must leave soon, but it has been just lovely. Seeing Easter and Martha, the last living passenger pigeons, was such a privilege. Thank you very much for inviting me to the event. Joe, please ensure the zoo looks after them, as I know you will."

"I'm going to check on them right now before I head out," Joe said.

Fran watched as he walked over to the aviary, hands in his pockets. Seamus caught up with Joe and walked beside him.

Mr. Finkel strolled over and stood next to Fran.

"Seamus has gotten tall," she said.

"Mm, he has. So, what did your mother have to say in her letter?"

She didn't answer him. Unlike the note of condolence from Joe, which comforted her, the letter from her mother terrified Fran.

"She's not well," her father said. "When you read it, take into consideration where she is now."

"Well, she's probably better off than most people are," Fran replied. "At least she knows she has a problem. I admire her for recognizing it. It's brave to do something society doesn't find acceptable, and women are judged harshly for it. I respect someone willing to risk doing something they believe is the right thing to do, even if it means sacrificing your reputation. None of us has a perfect mind," she continued, "if we did, we would only think positive thoughts all the time…and we don't. Nobody does."

They watched the crowd leaving.

Fran sighed. "I haven't even opened it yet. I'm afraid of what it may say. It's frightening, the power of words. Sometimes I feel like burning the letter. I'd rather jump out of a plane that's on fire than read what she wrote."

"Would you like me to read the letter for you?" her father asked.

Fran thought about it for a moment. "Thank you, Papa. But I think I'll wait until I find the courage to do it myself."

THE END

AUTHOR'S NOTE

Frances Finkel and the Passenger Pigeon is a work of historical fiction inspired by actual events and several real people, as well as birds.

"Project Peanut" is based on the Women's Auxiliary Ferrying Squadron (WAFS), an effort organized in 1942 and overseen by Nancy Love. The group of commercially rated pilots comprised less than thirty women, who ranged in age from 21 to 35. Members of the WAFS were required to have at least 500 hours of flying time as pilots in command. They were the first female pilots to ferry just about every type of aircraft flown in the U.S. Army Air Force during World War II, thus freeing up male pilots for fighting overseas. Cornelia Fort was the first woman to die in military service during WWII. The WAFS later merged with the Women Airforce Service Pilots (WASP). Female flyers were sensationalized by the press but rejected by most of the public; thus, Congress refused to approve them for military combat due to the heated controversy it drew. It was not until 1977 that these women pilots received full veteran status. In 2009, President Obama awarded them the Congressional Gold Medal.

The pigeoneer initiative was another little-known program of the era; the pigeon exploits described are inspired by real happenings. Colonel Clifford A. Poutré was the U.S. Army Signal Corps Chief Pigeoneer. He believed in using kindness to train pigeons and not the prior used method of starvation.

Maria Dickin founded the People's Dispensary for Sick Animals of the poor, a veterinarian charity in the U.K. She also instituted the "PDSA Dickin Medal" to acknowledge outstanding acts of bravery by animals serving in WWII.

The first recipients of the Dickin Medal were pigeons.

Known as the "Angel of the Delta," Margaret Haughery dedicated her entire life to working with the orphans of New Orleans. Once considered to be canonized as a saint, a monument in her honor can be found in the Lower Garden district of the city.

Martha lived at the Cincinnati Zoo and was believed to be the last passenger pigeon in existence. The zoo offered a generous reward to anyone who found another. No one did. She died alone in 1914.

The disappearance of a species once numbering in the billions sounded the alarm for animal activists, resulting in the passing of laws for the future protection of species and the creation of worldwide conservation organizations.

ABOUT THE AUTHOR

D.M. MAHONEY is both a helicopter and fixed wing rated pilot. She is a graduate of Northwestern University's Medill school of journalism and a member of the Historical Novel Society. Originally from the Dorchester neighborhood of Boston, Massachusetts, Mahoney currently resides in the Pacific Northwest region of the United States. This is her first novel.